G000123372

# MASTERS OF HEX

## A SUPERNATURAL SPEAKEASY MYSTERY
## BOOK THIRTEEN

## LILY HARPER HART

HARPERHART PUBLICATIONS

# 1

## ONE

"Absolutely not."

Zacharias "Zach" Sully took one look at the photo his fiancée, Ofelia Archer, had pulled up on her phone and immediately started shaking his head. He shook it so hard in fact, Ofelia was surprised it didn't fly right off his shoulders.

"Come on," she pleaded.

"No." Sully was firm.

"Please." She batted her eyelashes as she leaned closer to him. They were on stools—thankfully ones that had backs—and positioned at her brother Felix's bar as he tested new drink recipes. It was her night off, and she was determined to have fun. Sure, her idea of "fun" constituted torturing her future husband with a nonstop litany of photos. She wasn't sorry, though.

"It's not happening." Sully sipped his Sazerac and glared at the woman he loved more than anything. "Don't even think about it. I am not dressing up in tights."

"They're not tights," Ofelia shot back as she shook her phone. They'd been arguing about potential Halloween costumes for what felt like forever. In real time, it was probably only thirty minutes. It felt like years for both of them, however. "They're leggings."

"That's the same thing," Sully argued.

"It is not remotely the same thing."

"It is." Sully looked to Felix for help. The secondary Archer sibling was more apt to take Ofelia's side on important topics. This argument was small and petty, however, and that meant Felix was far more likely to take Sully's side.

Plus, well, Felix absolutely adored terrorizing his sister.

"Tell her that dressing up like Romeo is stupid," Sully ordered as Felix shoved a drink in front of him.

"Drink that," Felix said.

Sully made a face. "I'm not done with my current drink ... and I'm not twenty-two any longer. I have to moderate my drinking, or I'll have a hangover tomorrow."

"You're such a whiner," Felix muttered as he shook his head. "Maybe that means you would look good in tights."

"Shut up!" Sully jabbed a finger in Felix's direction. "I'm not dressing up like Romeo."

"But look at the dress," Ofelia argued as she gestured toward the woman standing next to the man in the Romeo costume in the photo. "Isn't the dress beautiful?"

Sully studied it for a moment, then shook his head. "I like my women in jeans and Converse."

"And I like them in spandex," Felix added.

Ofelia scowled at both of them. "I'm not saying that it's something I would want to wear on a regular basis—or even more than once—but it's so pretty." Ofelia's lower lip came out to play. That was normally a death sentence for Sully. He couldn't tell her no when she pulled out the big lip. "I would feel pretty in it."

On another day, when dealing with a bigger problem,

Sully might acquiesce and give her what she wanted. This was not that day, however.

"I'm not wearing tights." He took another sip of his Sazerac and ignored the pointed look Felix gave him regarding the new cocktail. Ever since Felix had won a drink contest against his sister a few weeks before, he'd been on a mission to create the next "big thing" in the French Quarter. While Sully admired the effort, he was over the weird cocktail concoctions. "You can wear the dress if you want," he added. "The thing is, baby, you always look beautiful." He beamed at Ofelia, who would've normally gone weak in the knees over a declaration like that.

Instead, she glowered at him. "We're wearing a couple's costume," she said. There was no give to her tone. "I finally have a boyfriend for Halloween, and we're coordinating costumes."

Sully had seemingly fallen head over heels for Ofelia the moment he'd met her. It had been love at first sight … or at least lust. He knew beyond a shadow of a doubt that she was his forever, and he couldn't wait to marry her.

This costume thing was a side of her he'd never expected, though.

"Why do we have to wear a couple's costume?" he demanded. "Stop waving that drink at me, Felix. I'll drink it when I want to drink it … and that might be never if you don't stop being obnoxious."

Felix made a whiny sound before stomping down toward the end of the bar to wait on some new customers.

Sully forced himself to suck in a breath, to calm himself, and then he pointed a relaxed smile toward his future wife. "I was thinking I would just put on a Dick Tracy hat and go as a cop."

Ofelia's disdain for the idea was obvious when she

made an exaggerated face. She was always expressive, but the way she rolled her eyes made Sully want to kiss her senseless. He wisely refrained, however.

"You're my first boyfriend," Ofelia explained.

"That is not even remotely true," Sully argued. "I've heard stories about your other boyfriends. I hate hearing those stories, but you dust them off when you want to irritate me. I know I'm not your one and only."

"You are now," Ofelia insisted.

"Maybe, but I haven't always been. Heck, we just locked away your last boyfriend because he was an evil turd. That's how your brother got this bar at such a good price."

"You mean that's how *you* got this bar for such a good price," Ofelia countered. "You're the one who owns it."

"Only until your brother pays me back, and he's not only been making his payments on time, but he's also been paying extra. Before you know it, the bar really will belong to Felix."

Ofelia stilled. "I didn't know that about the extra payments." A smile tipped the corners of her lips. "That's great."

Sully returned the grin. "It *is* great."

"We're still dressing in a couple's costume," Ofelia insisted. "Sebastian always worked Halloween night. He wouldn't go out with me." She gripped the front of Sully's shirt and pulled him toward her. "I need it!"

Sully was caught off guard by her vehemence. He was also a bit turned on. "I'm happy to give you whatever you need, Fe," he said in a sexy voice. "How about we finish up these drinks and head home so I can give you exactly what you need?"

Ofelia shot him a dubious look. "We're never going

home again until we decide on Halloween costumes. That means no sex for you."

Felix, who was just returning to check on his sister and Sully, made a horrified face. "How could you say that in front of me?"

Ofelia rolled her eyes. "Don't even. I've had to listen to your stories about the various women you've picked up from one corner of the Quarter to another since you were sixteen. You don't care that it makes me uncomfortable."

"Why would it make you uncomfortable?" Felix asked blankly.

"Why would this make you uncomfortable?" Ofelia shot back.

"Because you're my sister, and it's gross thinking about you having sex," Felix replied, not missing a beat. "You're a girl. I'm a boy. That means I'm allowed to talk about my sexploits. You're still a virgin in my head, though."

"That is unbelievably sexist," Ofelia complained.

"I don't care." Felix was having none of it. "When I look at him, I see a sexual predator." He jerked his thumb toward Sully. "That's not going to change."

"Yeah, yeah, yeah." Ofelia waved him off. She was calmer when she turned back to Sully. "I've always wanted to dress in a couple's costume for Halloween. Can't you please try? For me?"

The way her lower lip trembled—a deliberate choice on her part, Sully had no doubt—had him going soft inside.

"Fine," Sully muttered on a half grunt. "I'm not wearing tights, though."

"So, no period costumes," Ofelia mused. She focused on her phone again. She'd barely touched her cocktail because she'd been so fixated on picking out a costume. "What about Fred and Daphne?" She showed her screen to Sully.

Sully stared at the outfits for a beat and shook his head. "No. You would look great in that outfit—and, honestly, I think it would be hot if you wore a red wig for a night and those ridiculous boots ... and nothing else—but I've always felt that Fred was the most obnoxious one in the Scooby gang."

"He really was," Felix agreed. "Well, Velma was a close second."

"If you want me to dress up like Shaggy and you go as Daphne, I could maybe get behind that." Even as he made the offer, Sully wrinkled his nose to show how he really felt about the possibility.

"That doesn't work," Ofelia countered. "Shaggy and Daphne were never a couple."

"You could dress up like Scooby. Shaggy and Scooby were sort of a couple."

If looks could kill, Sully knew he would be dead. He swallowed hard before grabbing his Sazerac and throwing the rest back. He was smiling again when he handed the empty glass to Felix. "Let's come up with something else. There has to be something we both like."

Ofelia didn't look convinced, but she went back to focusing on her phone. "What about Raggedy Andy and Raggedy Ann? They make adorable yarn wigs, and the makeup is to die for."

Sully's mouth dropped open. "Do you actually want me to answer that question?" he demanded when Felix bent over at the waist and started laughing.

"Fred and Wilma?" Ofelia suggested.

"I'm not wearing a dress," Sully replied. "And, before you call me sexist or a misogynist or whatever, you should know that the odds of running into the people in my department are high that night. I don't want to make my own work environment torturous."

"You're basically saying cops are sexist jerks," Ofelia noted.

"I can't change the whole department, Fe," Sully replied. "I'm doing my best." To prove it, he pulled out his phone to start looking. He was determined to find something that wasn't ridiculous. "Hey, look here." He held up his phone so she could see the costume he'd found. "I can be a tequila bottle and you can be a lime wedge."

Outrage the likes he'd never seen before crossed Ofelia's face. "Are you kidding me right now? You'd better be kidding me."

Her tone told him to keep on scrolling. "We could be peanut butter and jelly." He tilted his screen so she could see the bread costumes. One side had what looked to be peanut butter spread on it. The other side had pink jelly everywhere.

"You're going to sleep on the couch tonight," Ofelia warned.

It was an empty threat—they both knew it—but Sully was starting to have fun winding her up. She would be feisty when it was time to go home, and there was little he loved more than his fiancée when she was feeling feisty. "So if peanut butter and jelly is off the table, I'm guessing the salsa and chip costume is a no-go," he mused, mostly to himself. "The same for the vending machine and the quarter."

"No food!" Ofelia practically bellowed.

"Food is out," Sully said as he kept on scrolling. "Oh, look, we could be Wayne and Garth." He was actually excited about that prospect, but Ofelia's narrowed eyes told him that was a mistake. "I loved *Wayne's World*," he explained in a soft voice.

"I'm not wearing jeans on Halloween," Ofelia gritted out.

"Good grief," Sully muttered as he went back to his phone search. "I don't understand why you're so intense about this. Although ... look." He held up his phone again. "I could be the hot dog and you could be the bun."

"That's not phallic or anything," Felix mused, shaking his head. In truth, he was enjoying watching his sister and her fiancé fight over something as trivial as Halloween costumes. Ofelia was so happy she had to manufacture fights now. He wanted her happy more than anything, and even though he found Sully annoying at times, he felt as if they'd all formed a close-knit family unit over the past year.

"It's because she didn't win the high school costume contest," Felix volunteered, changing the subject on the fly.

"What's because she didn't win the high school costume contest?" Sully asked blankly. He was officially confused.

"This freak-out of hers." Felix pushed the new cocktail in front of Sully yet again. "Drink that or you're not getting anything else."

Sully made a face, but he grabbed the cocktail. "I'll drink it if you tell me about the Halloween costume contest," he offered.

"Deal." Felix grinned as Ofelia made a protesting sound with her tongue.

"Don't tell that story," Ofelia warned. "I'll make you cry if you try."

"Oh, it's cute that you think I'm afraid of you," Felix teased. "I'm not, though."

"Just really quick," Sully interjected. "This costume

makes you look like a socket and my costume would have a plug to fit into your socket, and it just so happens to be near where my crotch would be." He waited a beat. "No?"

"I can't even look at you I'm so grossed out," Ofelia lamented.

Sully chuckled. He wasn't surprised that was her response. "Tell me about the Halloween costume contest," he instructed Felix as he went back to looking.

"We had a Halloween costume contest when we were in high school," Felix replied. "The grand prize was a hundred bucks and a huge bag of Snickers. I think Fe wanted the Snickers as much as the hundred bucks."

"Don't ever talk to me again," Ofelia growled.

Felix knew she didn't mean it, so he continued. "Ofelia has always had a thing about Halloween. It's been her favorite holiday since we were kids and we saw one of the *Friday the 13th* movies on AMC. We weren't supposed to be watching, but we did anyway, and she fell in love with being scared while watching the movie. Then she got into Halloween as a byproduct because of watching the movie."

"You're completely off on a tangent," Ofelia complained.

"You kind of are," Sully agreed.

"I'm laying the groundwork," Felix countered. "I just need you to understand that Ofelia is nutty about Halloween, and she's not going to let this couple's costume idea go."

"Duly noted." Sully sipped the new cocktail and cocked his head. "Is that mint?"

"Yeah." Felix rubbed his hands together. "And chocolate liquor. What do you think?"

"It tastes like a Girl Scout Cookie."

"Is that a bad thing?"

"No, but I'm not sure this is the sort of cocktail you can drink over and over again in the same night," Sully replied. "People like to pick a cocktail and stick to it when getting drunk. People come to the French Quarter to get drunk." He let Felix deduce the rest.

"Therefore, I need drinks that people want to drink ten of on the same night," Felix realized.

"There it is." Sully bobbed his head. "This is good though. It's ... interesting. It's better for a dinner party, though."

"Okay. Okay." Felix bobbed his head and jotted down a few notes on a pad he was keeping behind the bar. "Where was I?"

"You were done telling the story," Ofelia replied.

"No, you were just getting to the part about Ofelia dressing up for a high school contest," Sully countered.

"Right." Felix finished jotting down his notes and snagged gazes with Sully. "Ofelia didn't always get along with all the girls in our school. We went to one of the nicer schools, but we didn't have as much money as the other kids. Our parents got a break on our tuition because my dad knew a lot of drunks and a few of them happened to be rich drunks."

"I get it." Sully's hand landed on Ofelia's back. He'd assumed this was going to be a funny story. Now he wasn't so certain. Either way, he wanted to hear it.

"The other girls had these elaborate Halloween costumes," Felix explained. "Their parents spent thousands of dollars on these fairy tale princess dresses. One of them dressed up like Barbie and had seven-hundred-dollar boots."

"That sounds like a complete and total waste of money," Sully noted.

"Oh, it was," Felix agreed. "Ofelia wanted to be one of the kids who got to dress up and wow everybody for one night. My dad didn't believe in spending that sort of money, though, so Ofelia made her own costume."

"I learned how to sew in home economics," Ofelia explained. "I thought since I'd sewn a pillow, I could sew a costume. I was wrong."

"She got a pattern from the craft store, and saved up for the fabric, and worked really hard to make a dress so she could be Cinderella like some of the other girls," Felix continued.

Sully darted a worried look toward Ofelia. He was starting to hate this story. "I don't want to hear this if something bad happened," he said.

"You don't hear me touting the time I won the Halloween costume contest ever, do you?" Ofelia demanded.

"Ugh."

"My seams were bad, and the dress ripped when I was trying to dance in it," Ofelia replied. "Like ... the dress completely fell apart. I was horrified, and I had to hide in the bathroom until my mother showed up with something for me to change into. Only she had one of her social meetings that night..." Ofelia trailed off.

"Suffice it to say that I had to give her my gym clothes, so she had something to go home in," Felix volunteered. He was clearly amused by the story, but Ofelia didn't look happy.

"Show me the Romeo costume again," Sully demanded when his stomach had finished squirming over the thought of Ofelia hiding in the bathroom and blotting tears for hours, her Cinderella dress in pieces and falling off of her. The fact that her mother couldn't be bothered to leave a party to help her only daughter was so on-brand for Marie Charles that he wanted to find her and shake her.

"No, you don't want to wear leggings," Ofelia reminded him.

"I want to make you happy more than I care about the leggings." Even saying it made him cringe when he pictured the uniforms in his department getting a gander of him when he was out carousing with Ofelia that night. He was resigned to endless months of torture.

"No." Ofelia placed her hand on his wrist and shook her head. "We'll figure out something else."

Sully glanced over to gauge if she was being a martyr. "I'll put in more effort to pick a legit costume idea," he said finally. "I really did think the socket one was awesome, though."

Ofelia rolled her eyes. "I don't want something sexual. I want something that's cool but depicts a real couple."

"Like ... Princess Diana and Charles are a real couple, or like Ariel and Eric are a real couple? And, before you answer that, know that I would prefer we stay away from the Disney princesses when choosing. I just ... please go with something else."

"First off, if we were going to dress like Diana and Charles, there would probably be a knife involved or something," she said. "As for Disney princesses, I'm okay staying away from them. I want something good, though. I want to look beautiful."

"Baby, you always look beautiful," Sully insisted.

"Well, I want to look extra beautiful this year," Ofelia said. "I need you to get with the program."

"Fine." Sully was determined to pick something that didn't make him want to wretch, but his phone dinged with an incoming message, and he got distracted.

"What is it?" Ofelia asked as he read his screen.

"There's a body behind the art studio over on Royal Street," he replied as he stood. He was rueful as he regarded her. "I have to head over there to check it out."

"Murder?" Felix asked.

Sully shrugged. "Right now, it's just a body. Unfortunately, because this is the French Quarter, we have more than a few people drink themselves to death on any given month. It could be accidental. It could be natural causes. It could be a wife slamming her husband over the head with a frying pan."

Ofelia perked up. "We could be Desi and Lucy."

He considered it for a second, then shrugged. "We'll make a list." He leaned in and kissed her. "I'll let you know if I'm going to be late coming home tonight once I get a look at the scene. Are you okay to get home?"

"I haven't even finished a single drink," Ofelia replied. "I've been too busy looking at costumes."

"Be careful anyway." Sully gave her another kiss. "I'll be in touch."

"I'll have a list started when I see you again."

Sully had no doubt. "Won't that be fun?"

# 2
## TWO

"You can help me pick out a couple's costume," Ofelia said to Felix once Sully was gone. Even though her fiancé wasn't keen on the idea, she was determined to come up with something that was out of this world.

"Oh, it's only fun when I can torture Sully with the possibilities," Felix whined. "He's gone. He might not come back after the Romeo costume either."

Ofelia made a face. "Don't give him grief," she warned. "If you make it hard on him, he's going to make it hard on me."

"We can't have that," Felix teased.

"I want a couple's costume," Ofelia insisted. "There's that big street party happening this year, and I want to look good."

"Big street party?" Felix looked momentarily confused. When realization dawned on his handsome features, Ofelia looked away. "Are we talking about the street party where all the people from our high school are scheduled to meet up?" he asked sagely.

"Hmm?" Ofelia was suddenly fascinated with the cocktail she'd allowed to go watery.

Disgusted, Felix snagged it from her and dumped it before starting to mix a fresh one. "That's what you're talking about, right? That group of mean girls is supposed to be coming this year. I saw it in the little Facebook group they created for the party."

"I have no idea what you're talking about," Ofelia lied.

"Uh-huh." Felix didn't believe her for a second.

"I don't," Ofelia insisted. "I just ... want to look pretty along with my fiancé."

"Who happens to be from a really rich family, and who bought you a rock the size of your head when he proposed."

"I don't care about stuff like that." Ofelia was scandalized. "You know money isn't important to me."

"Says the woman who bought a second building and is shaping herself into an entrepreneur," Felix drawled.

"If they want to admire me because I'm a smart businesswoman, I'm fine with that," Ofelia said. "I don't care about the actual money though."

"Then what do you care about?" Felix was honestly curious.

"Zach is way hotter than any guy they could've gotten," Ofelia replied. "He needs the perfect costume to show off his hotness."

"And there it is." Felix was amused despite himself. "That is so shallow, Fe. You really want to show off your fiancé's hotness?"

"Of course I do. He's amazing. They're treating this Halloween party as a mini reunion of sorts. Sully is going to look good for it if I have to magically force him into an appropriate costume and drag him there by a magical leash."

Felix burst out laughing. "That is ... so you." He swiped at errant laughter tears when he'd finished. "Although, you do bring up a good point." He was suddenly serious. "I run my own bar now. I wasn't planning on going to that party, but maybe I should. All those people who said I was unfocused and wouldn't amount to anything owe me an apology."

"They do," Ofelia agreed. "What are you going to dress up as?"

"I don't know. That's a good question. What do you think?" Felix was seemingly intent.

"You need something that shows you're powerful," Ofelia mused. "Maybe you could do something from *The Godfather*. You would look good as a mobster."

"I *would* look good as a mobster," Felix readily agreed. "I was thinking something along the lines of *Magic Mike*, though."

Ofelia's frown was instantaneous. "The stripper movie?"

"Hey, I'm powerful and look great without a shirt on," Felix argued. "I should take advantage of both of those things."

"If you say so." Ofelia wasn't impressed. "You can't go to the Halloween party without a shirt. You'll draw too much attention."

"That's exactly why I'm doing it. I—" Felix broke off when he realized Ofelia had gripped the bar out of nowhere. She looked as if she were holding on for dear life, even though there was no reason she would fall off her stool. "Fe?" He took a concerned step forward.

Ofelia gripped the bar so tightly that she felt it was possible she might break off a chunk. There was a noise in her head, a clanging sound, and all she knew with any degree of certainty was that Sully was in trouble.

No voices spelled it out for her. No images assailed her mind. The only thing she felt was unadulterated fear for Sully as her heart pounded and threatened to rip right out of her chest.

Slowly, as if wading through quicksand, Ofelia climbed off the stool. She had to keep a grip on the bar to keep herself upright, but she managed to land on her feet.

"What are you doing?" Felix demanded. There wasn't a single trace of mirth on his features. He knew when Ofelia was messing around, and she would never make him think there was something wrong with her as part of a joke. That's not how it worked in their family, thanks to their father's mental illness. "What's happening?"

"Zach." That was all Ofelia could initially say. She had to force out the rest. "Zach is in trouble."

Felix looked caught. "He's with other cops. He should be fine."

"No."

Ofelia pushed herself away from the bar, her gaze moving toward the door. "He needs me."

"I'll go with you." Felix was already untying his apron when Ofelia shook her head and caught his eye. "I can't let you go alone," he protested when he realized she was going to try to keep him from heading out with her.

"You can't go with me." Ofelia was firm on that. "You'll be another distraction. Just wait here. I'll be fine." She wasn't worried about herself. Sully was a different story, however. She only made it two steps before she stilled. "He said he was going to the art gallery over on Royal, right?"

"He said there was a body behind the art gallery on

Royal," Felix replied. "There's only one problem with that, though, Fe."

Ofelia already knew what the problem was. She didn't need to be reminded.

"There are eight art galleries over there," Felix hissed.

Ofelia nodded. She was already resigned to what had to be done. "I'll find him."

"What if you don't?"

"That's not an option." What Ofelia didn't say was that there was no doubt that if she didn't find Sully, he wouldn't survive the night. She wouldn't allow that.

No, they were destined for happily ever after. She would die to protect that.

**FELIX'S BAR WAS ONLY A FEW BLOCKS AWAY FROM** Royal Street. That meant Ofelia managed to make it over there within a few minutes. Once she hit the intersection of Conti and Royal, however, she was at a loss.

She didn't know whether to go right or left.

The crowd out in the French Quarter was light this evening, and it was something Ofelia was grateful for. The run-up to Halloween was normally busy on Bourbon Street, but things shifted after that. The Quarter got a break from the party shenanigans to regroup and boost their flagging energy before starting it all over again after the first of the year as they braced for Mardi Gras to hit again. Some business owners hated the downtime. Ofelia was a fan because it allowed her a chance to breathe.

Breathing wasn't something that was coming easy at this time, however. All she could think was that if she turned in the wrong direction, she would lose Sully forever.

She went with her instincts and moved to her right.

Something inside of her, something that appealed to her witchy sensibilities, pulled her in that direction. She only made it half a block before she was rewarded with movement out of the corner of her eye. When she darted her gaze in that direction, she saw what was clearly a man moving from the street to the sidewalk.

She opened her mouth to call out to Sully even though, deep down, she knew it wasn't him. Then she cocked her head when she realized the man appeared to be dancing. That was the only word she could think to describe what she was seeing.

He was dressed in black pants and a white and black striped top. He wore black suspenders and white gloves. And, as he grew closer, she realized his face was covered in white and black makeup. He'd topped off the entire outfit with a black bowler hat.

"Well, that's just weird," Ofelia said as the mime—because that's clearly what she was dealing with—danced under one of the gas-powered streetlights.

As if finally realizing that he wasn't alone, the mime turned and met her gaze. He seemed to expect to find her standing there. When he waved and smiled, Ofelia felt a chill going down her spine.

This wasn't right. She had no idea why she was so determined it was wrong, however.

"Have you seen anybody out here?" she called out. The echo of her voice made her realize that Royal Street was well and truly dead. If she'd been trapped in a zombie movie, this was about the time when a horde would've come trucking out of one of the alleys and killed her. It wasn't that Royal Street was always bustling with activity. It wasn't Bourbon Street after all. It was never this dead, though, either. "Are you alone?" she asked as the mime started a tap dance routine to music only he could seemingly hear.

In response, the mime pretended to be trapped inside of an invisible box. That only served to grate on Ofelia all the more.

"Listen." She took a step forward, her temper flaring, and then she caught more movement. This time it was across the street, near the entrance to an alley. She snapped her head in that direction and found another mime—this one a bit wider and rounder—performing a similar routine.

Now, if this had been another city, one that didn't have the colorful history of New Orleans to call on, Ofelia might have been spooked. And, yes, the mimes were freaky in their own way. She was a child of the French Quarter, though. It was going to take a lot more than a few mimes to frighten her.

"Enough of this." Ofelia lashed out with her magic and sent the mime that was closest to the alley flying. It hadn't escaped her attention that the alley the dancing monstrosity was protecting happened to be behind an art gallery. Sure, this was the art gallery where the artist randomly stuck boobs into the background of famous paintings and sold them for fifty bucks a pop, but it was still technically an art gallery.

Ofelia didn't stop to see if the mime she'd thrown out of the way was okay. Instead, she barreled into the alley with a purpose, determined to save Sully if he'd been backed into a corner by rabid mimes.

What she found had her making a sputtering noise as she took it in.

There were at least ten—probably more—mimes forming a circle in the middle of the alley area. It was more of a patio than an alley. Well, other than the dumpster.

What was important from her perspective was that there was no secondary outlet. Ofelia ignored the smell of garbage, and the closed-in feeling that was threatening to smother her and focused on the thing in the middle of the circle.

Sully was face down and unmoving on the pavement. Ofelia couldn't see any blood, or a knife sticking out of his back, but that didn't necessarily mean anything. He was down, not moving, and there was what looked to be a nasty bruise flourishing on his cheek. From this distance, she couldn't tell if he was breathing. If he wasn't, she had every intention of setting every mime that had gathered on fire.

"Get away," she roared as she threw out her hand and flung a huge wall of magic at the mimes. The wave was big enough to cast all of them aside as if they were bowling pins and she was going for a perfect game.

Ofelia's feet pounded on the uneven courtyard pavement as she hurried to Sully. He'd yet to move, and when she crouched next to him, all she could do was whisper the same fervent prayer over and over again.

*Please let him be all right. Don't let him leave. I can't make it without him.*

When she pressed her fingers to Sully's neck, she almost cried out in relief when she felt the steady beat of his pulse. The breath she hadn't even realized she'd been holding escaped, and she briefly closed her eyes.

Then she remembered the mimes.

When she lifted her chin and looked, she found that the mimes had regained their footing. Some looked a little worse for wear thanks to them flying through the air and slamming into walls. They all appeared to be annoyed with her greeting.

"What do you want?" Ofelia demanded as she looked

between them. There was magic present. She could feel it, but it was hard for her to identify what sort of magic she was dealing with. "What are you?" she asked the nearest mime.

He cocked his head, stared hard into her eyes, and showed his teeth. They were pointed, and he made a growling noise.

Because she was at the end of her rope—Sully might have been breathing, but he still wasn't awake—Ofelia narrowed her eyes and unleashed the sort of magic that sent children screaming and running to their parents.

"*Ango*," she gritted out. A black gush of magic rushed out of nowhere and tackled the mime to the ground. Even when hitting with the force of a full tilt train, the mime didn't make a sound. The only noise came when a bone snapped, and the mime raised its chin in anguish. It didn't scream, but it was almost as if Ofelia could feel it screaming.

"Go away," she intoned when the mime turned its angry eyes to her. "Just ... go away. Believe it or not, I have no interest in keeping this up. I don't want to kill you. I just want you gone."

The mime did not respond. Instead, it ignored the arm that hung uselessly on its left side and began to pretend to be in a box with the right arm.

Rather than feel pity for the creature, Ofelia's annoyance ramped up. "Are you trying to make me kill you?" she growled. "Enough is enough." She raised her hand to throw out another bolt of magic. This time she was determined to kill one of them in the hope that the others would flee in the aftermath. Before she could unleash her magic, however, a new sound joined the mix of scampering feet in the alley.

Slowly—so slowly Ofelia felt as if she were trying to react while covered in fast-drying cement—she turned her eyes to the opening that led to the street. She didn't know what she was expecting, although more mimes wasn't out of the question. The one thing she certainly didn't expect, however, was the big black panther that was padding down the center of the walkway.

It was bigger than almost anything she'd ever seen, and that included Sully when he was in his panther form. It had huge paws, sleek fur, and bright eyes. It made a chuffing sound as it trotted into the alley, and then it plopped itself down directly in front of Ofelia.

"Hello," she said dumbly. She recognized she wasn't dealing with a real panther. This wasn't some wild animal that had escaped from the zoo. It was a shifter, just like Sully, and it was here because it was apparently taking her side in the fight with the mimes. Despite that, the creature didn't speak ... and it didn't move on the mimes.

"While I'm happy to see you, I'm not sure that sitting here and doing nothing is the way to go," Ofelia said as she checked Sully's breathing one more time. "I believe we need to clear this alley if we want to be able to move forward. Do you think you're up for that?"

The panther didn't consider it long. In fact, it only sat still until one of the mimes reached out to poke it. Then it swiped out with one of those huge paws, aiming for the poking mime, and almost ripped its arm clean off.

Alarm ripped through the mimes, although they had yet to utter a single word. Two of them lurched toward Ofelia, but she sent out a killing curse that ripped them both to shreds in an instant. By the time she was finished, they were completely gone. You couldn't even tell they'd been there.

That was the tipping point. The other mimes backed down the aisle that led to freedom. They eyed the panther and Ofelia with a great deal of disgust, and there was a warning in their glares. They were essentially telling the duo this wasn't over.

"Whenever you're ready for a real fight, I'll be here, you jerkwads," Ofelia shot back, flipping them the bird before dropping to sit next to Sully. He was still breathing, his chest rising and falling at regular intervals, but he'd yet to open his eyes. "Zach, can you wake up for me?" Her voice was gentle, and she was careful when looking for a wound. All she could find was a bump on the back of his head, though. They'd clearly hit him with something.

Next to her, the panther shifted into human form. He was an older man, although distinguished. He was also buck naked, and he was breathing heavily as he dragged a hand through his silver hair to organize it.

"Nice penis," Ofelia said as she determinedly kept her eyes on Sully. She didn't look because it wasn't polite. And, well, she had other things to worry about.

"It is very nice," the shifter agreed. "I've gotten compliments on it for as long as I can remember."

"How great for you." Ofelia wasn't in the mood to have this conversation.

"Is he okay?" the shifter asked, inclining his head toward Sully.

"He will be if I can get him home," Ofelia replied. Her mind was already working. "I have a salve that will help him. I just don't know how I'm going to get him there."

"I can help," the shifter replied. He was surprisingly calm despite the circumstances.

"Naked?" Ofelia demanded. "You're going to help when you're naked?"

"My clothes are at the other end of the alley," he replied on a chuckle. "That's where I shifted."

"Oh." Ofelia wasn't certain what to say. "I can call my brother."

"That won't be necessary, Ofelia."

She froze in place. How did he know her name? "Who are you?" she demanded. She wasn't keen on another fight, but she would embrace it if necessary. "Just who the hell are you?"

"Topher Sully," he replied as he extended his hand. "You can call me Zeke, though. Everybody does."

Ofelia deflated like a leaky balloon. "Topher Sully?" She couldn't believe it.

Zeke nodded. "I believe that's my son unconscious on the ground."

"Of course it is." Ofelia didn't have the energy to marvel at this turn of events. "It wouldn't be October in the Quarter if I didn't get to see a random guy naked."

"Miracles come in all shapes and sizes," he agreed. "I'll get my clothes. Then we can get him home. After that ... we'll figure it out. How does that sound?"

Ofelia didn't have a choice in the matter. "It sounds great. I'll be right here while you're covering ... all of that." She waved her hand and looked away.

Zeke chuckled. "I didn't know you were such a prude. This should be fun, though."

That wasn't the word Ofelia would've used for the situation. She was beyond it, though. "Get dressed. The sooner I treat him, the better."

"Your wish is my command."

# 3
## THREE

Zeke was calm when he returned, smiling at Ofelia reassuringly. He showed none of the gentleness Ofelia would've preferred when grabbing Sully under the arms and pulling him to his feet, however.

"There's no crime in being gentle," she growled as she tried to slide under Sully's arm. She had no idea how she was going to drag him back to Krewe, the bar she owned, and they lived over together, but she was determined to try.

Zeke gave her a pointed look. "Honey, I believe that a woman can do anything a man can do," he started.

"Did you just call me honey?" Ofelia was incensed.

Zeke ignored the question. "In this particular instance, I don't think you're capable of carrying my son home. He's dead weight ... and you're an itty-bitty thing."

Ofelia glared at him. "I am not itty-bitty. Don't call me honey either. I don't like it."

Rather than be offended—Zeke was a rich and powerful man after all—he grinned at her. "You're adorable. Has anybody ever told you that?"

Ofelia was about to tell him where he could stuff his

opinion when footsteps on the pavement distracted her. "I swear, if those freaking mimes are back, I'm shredding every single one of them," she groused as she turned to fight whoever was descending on their location. To her surprise, she found a vampire sliding into the alley. He was a familiar one at that. "Pascal?"

Pascal Fontaine was something of a second father to Ofelia. When she was a child, he helped her father carry her through a flooding French Quarter to get her to safety during Hurricane Katrina. As an adult, he'd swooped in to get her out of trouble more than once when she'd gotten in over her head.

She'd never been as excited to see anybody in her entire life. "What are you doing here?" Ofelia tried to take a step toward him, but she was still holding up Sully and, much as she didn't want to admit it, Zeke was right. She couldn't carry him even a single step.

Pascal took in the situation for a beat, then shrugged. "Someone said there were mimes over here. I happen to love a good mime."

Ofelia made a face. "Mimes are creepy."

"I didn't say I was going to hang around with them." Pascal showed her his fangs, as a joke probably, and then turned to Zeke. "And there's a face I haven't seen in quite some time."

Zeke smiled. "Did you miss me?"

"About as much as the mimes." Pascal let loose a heavy breath as he regarded the shifter. "I thought you were spending all your time up in Baton Rouge these days."

"You can't be a proper Louisiana businessman and never visit the French Quarter," Zeke replied. "Besides, my son does live here ... and he's recently engaged. What makes you think I'm not here to meet my future daughter-in-law?"

Pascal's response was to snort. Then he moved in closer to get a look at Sully. "What happened here?"

"He got a call about a dead body," Ofelia replied. "We were at Archer. I had a ... *feeling* ... that he was in trouble. I came looking and there were mimes everywhere."

"I heard the mimes were hunting," Pascal said. "I wanted to check it out myself. I had no idea they were hunting you." He looked disturbed at the prospect.

"Not me." Ofelia shook her dark head. "Zach. He got a text. I saw it."

"Well, we'll deal with that when we get him out of here." Pascal took a step toward him. "I'm assuming you have something to fix his head injury at home."

"I have healing potions," Ofelia agreed. "He's heavy, though."

"I'll take him." Pascal slid his arm around Sully's waist. He shot Zeke a dark look when the shifter refused to release his son. "You can't just toss him over your back and carry him through the Quarter," he said reasonably. "The police will question you, and I'm not sure that 'we fought off a mime attack' is going to work since you'll be carrying a police officer. They'll recognize him."

Ofelia's innards clutched. "He's right. We have to let him take him."

"And how are you going to take him without anybody noticing?" Zeke demanded.

Pascal lifted his chin toward the rooftop. "Nobody will see me. I can take him in through the patio on the second floor. It will be quick and efficient."

Ofelia nodded. "That's the way it has to be." She was

resigned. "When you get him there, put him in bed. There are healing potions in the medicine cabinet."

"Are they marked as such?"

"No, but they're purple."

"I'll wait for you for that part," Pascal replied. "It's not as if you'll be far behind. You're only a couple blocks from home."

Ofelia was reticent to leave Sully's side, but she knew it was best for him. "I'll see you soon," she whispered as she kissed his cheek. She had to fight the urge to cry when she pulled back. "Take care of him," she ordered Pascal. "If you see mimes, don't stay and fight because you want to crush them. Get him to safety first."

"He'll be fine," Pascal reassured her. His gaze was heavy when it landed on Zeke. "You make sure she gets home safely."

"I don't need a babysitter," Ofelia growled.

Pascal ignored her. "I'm taking your family to safety. Mine had better arrive without a hair out of place."

Zeke cocked his head as he glanced between Ofelia and the vampire. He ultimately nodded. "She's going to be my daughter-in-law. Of course I'll take care of her."

"See that you do." With that, Pascal swept Sully over his shoulder, and then leaped to the roof of the nearest building. "I'll see you soon." He was gone into the night within seconds.

"Come on." Ofelia motioned for Zeke to follow her. Now that it was just the two of them, she had no choice but to deal with the man who had roared into her life in the midst of mimes and inopportune nudity. "It won't take us long to get there."

Zeke didn't put up a fight. Instead, he followed. He paid

special attention to Bourbon Street when they passed. "Light night," he mused.

"The weather is turning, and it's midweek," Ofelia replied. "Honestly, we're getting to the time of year when the locals get to take over for a few months."

"Right." Zeke seemed to be taking it all in. "You own a bar, correct?"

"Yes." Ofelia inclined her head toward the tunnel that led to Krewe when they got close to the opening. "I took over my father's bar."

"And he's crazy, correct?"

It took everything Ofelia had not to pop Zeke in the face. "Come on. There's no reason to go inside the bar. We'll take the side stairs up."

"I would kind of like to see where you work," Zeke argued. "You know, just so I can get a feel for you."

Ofelia was at the end of her rope. "Then go in there and have a drink. In fact, drink whatever you want on the house. Just tell the guy behind the bar who you are." She stomped as she started up the stairs.

"I take it that's not what you want," Zeke called after her.

"Do you care what I want?"

"I seem to have offended you."

Ofelia let loose a growling noise. "Do what you want. I'm going to make sure your son is okay."

"Yeah, I've definitely offended you. Sorry about that."

Ofelia ignored the apology. She had her key out when she reached the door, and she eagerly pushed inside. "Pascal?"

"I'm here," Pascal assured her. True to his word, he had Sully on the couch. He was sitting in a chair across from Sully and had Ofelia's black kitten—who was actually a full-grown cat now—on his lap as he stroked the feline. "Sully is still breathing," he assured her when he met her questioning gaze. "Don't worry."

"I'll get the potions," Ofelia said as she raced toward the bedroom.

Zeke was slow as he wandered into the apartment. He closed the door behind him out of habit more than concern for the cat getting loose, and then he proceeded to wander into the open kitchen so he could take a look around. "The floors are nice," he said after a beat. "They look as if they've been refinished recently." He opened the cupboards and looked inside. "The dishes could use an upgrade."

Pascal dressed down Zeke with a single look. "Sit down," he ordered.

Zeke arched an eyebrow. "Since when are you the boss of me?"

"This is your son's home," Pascal replied. "Show some respect."

"The boy doesn't show me much respect." Despite his words, Zeke trudged into the living room. "I've never given much thought to living above a bar, but now that I've seen the setup, it seems convenient." He lowered himself into the chair next to Pascal. "What's with the cat?"

"Baron," Pascal replied. His longer fingers were sending the feline into ecstasy as he stroked the black cat. "Ofelia adopted him right around the time she adopted your son."

"That's convenient," Zeke mused. "Zach has always been a sucker for an animal or human in need." His gaze landed on Ofelia as she hurried into the room with multiple tubes and bottles clutched to her chest. "Always."

"Be careful," Pascal warned in a low voice. "She is not weak, and I can hear the gears in your mind working. I'll end you if you do a single thing to upset her."

Rather than be offended, or act as if he cared in the least, Zeke merely smirked. "When did you become a parent?"

"I'm not her father. She has a father. I am, however, extremely fond of her. You should take that into consideration when you do ... whatever it is you've come here to do."

Ofelia had Sully's head resting against her chest when Zeke looked up. He was surprised she'd managed to lift him without anybody noticing. He watched with fascination as she upended the healing potion into his mouth, and then leaned forward as he waited for Sully to respond.

He didn't have to wait long.

Sully made a choking sound as he swallowed the potion Ofelia was pouring down his throat. When his eyes snapped open, confusion reigned as he tried to figure out exactly how he'd ended up on his couch, his fiancée's arms wrapped around him. "Ofelia?" he asked dumbly.

She nodded, her breath rushing out as she finally allowed a tear to fall. "Yeah. It's me. Are you okay?"

Sully's forehead creased with confusion as he took in the others in the room. Pascal was in the chair with Baron. And his father of all people was in the other chair. They were all watching him expectantly.

"Why do I feel as if I'm a contestant on a game show and I'm about to make the wrong guess?" he asked, his voice rusty.

"You're fine," Ofelia assured him. "I'm going to take care of you."

"Of course you are, baby." Sully absently patted the arm she had wrapped around him. He couldn't stop himself from focusing on his father, even as Ofelia turned her attention to the tender spot on the back of his head. He hissed when she poked at the bump, and then sighed when she poured her magical healing elixir on it. "Father," he said blandly.

"Zacharias." Zeke looked a little too amused with himself as he regarded his only son. "How are you feeling?"

"I'm fine." Sully moved to sit up, but Ofelia slapped his side.

"You need to rest," she insisted as she kept a firm grip on him.

Before falling in love with Ofelia, Sully would've had a problem with allowing someone else to keep control given the current circumstances. It was not allowed to look weak in front of a paternal figure in panther shifter circles. Sully had given up caring about that world a long time ago, however. He was more interested in making Ofelia feel safe than anything else. "Yes, baby," he said as he slumped against her. She was picking through his hair looking for more bumps, although it reminded him of monkeys looking for bugs to eat. He let it go, though. "I'm confused about what happened," he said after several seconds. "How did I get here?"

"What do you remember?" Pascal asked. He looked legitimately curious.

"Um ... I was at Archer with Ofelia and Felix."

"What's Archer?" Zeke queried.

"Ofelia's brother's bar," Sully replied. "We were having drinks and talking about couple's costumes for Halloween."

"Couple's costumes?" Zeke looked horrified. "You can't be serious."

"And just what's wrong with a couple's costume?" Ofelia demanded. She was officially at the end of her rope. She hated how shrill she sounded, but there was no holding back.

"Where do you want me to start?" Zeke queried.

"Don't." Sully jabbed a finger in his father's direction. "Just ... don't. Now is not the time to get her going."

"I was just sitting here," Zeke replied in innocent fashion. "I mean ... I am the one who rushed in and saved you. I think that means I've earned a little bit of love."

"You didn't save him," Ofelia argued. "I saved him."

"Um ... I'm the one who rushed in and scared off the mimes."

"And I'm the one who shredded two of them," she reminded him. "I was just getting ready to shred some more of them when you came in without any invitation. I had everything under control."

Sully ignored the brewing argument and concentrated on his memory. The word "mimes" had triggered something, and he was starting to get a picture of what happened. "The call about the body," he volunteered dully. "That was a lie. It was a trap. They were trying to draw me in. They were waiting for me."

Ofelia flicked her eyes to him. "You remember."

"I remember going to the alley," he replied. "I was confused. There were no lights. No cars around. No cops. I thought I'd made a mistake and gone to the wrong alley, but when I turned, I was surrounded."

Ofelia clutched him tighter. "It's okay. I saved you."

"Oh, you did not," Zeke countered. "I'm the one who saved the day."

"You're the one who showed me your penis," Ofelia shot back. "Let's get it right."

For the first time since he'd joined the party, Zeke had the grace to look embarrassed. "It was not how she's making it sound," he insisted to Sully, who looked as if he was ready to start throwing punches ... or maybe bullets. "I was in my alternative form when I rushed in to protect my only son. When I shifted back, obviously she saw ... the good stuff." He held out his hands and smiled. "It was an accident."

"Did he just say 'the good stuff'?" Ofelia demanded.

Because he was still struggling to figure out exactly how he'd managed to get where he was, Sully slid his arm around Ofelia and shifted their positions, essentially forcing her on top of him so he could hold her ... and maybe calm her down. Apparently, his father was doing what he did best and irritating her to the point of no return simply because he enjoyed doing it.

"Can you not drive her over the edge?" he demanded of his father. "As for you..." He trailed off as he took in Ofelia's pale features. She'd obviously been through an ordeal. "You I love," he said, whatever admonishment he'd been preparing to unleash dying on his lips. "I love you more than anything in fact." He kissed her forehead.

To everybody's surprise, he turned to Pascal. "Why don't you tell me what happened?" he suggested. "I think that's the wisest course."

Pascal's chuckle was light. "I'm not entirely certain what happened. I heard there were mimes running around acting weird. I've always hated mimes and wanted to see if I could mess with them. When I arrived, there were no mimes. There was just Ofelia and your father ... and they didn't seem to be playing all that nice."

"That's because I saw little Zeke, and he gave me serious side eye," Ofelia whispered.

Sully had to press his lips together to keep from laughing. "I've got it, baby." He stroked his hand over her hair. "How did you know to come?" he demanded of his father.

"I was just coming from dinner about two blocks over,"

Zeke replied. "It was a business dinner, and when we left the restaurant, I scented you."

"Wait ... you were in town on business and didn't tell Zach?" Ofelia demanded. "What's up with that?"

"I was going to contact him tomorrow," Zeke replied. "I figured I would be out late this evening, and I've been on three planes this week. Don't get run over by that judgmental express you've got going on there."

Ofelia's eye roll was pronounced. "Whatever," she muttered under her breath.

Sully chuckled as he continued to rub soothing circles against the back of her neck. "So, you just happened upon me?" he questioned his father.

"Pretty much," Zeke confirmed. "When I got there, Ofelia was next to you and struggling with what to do."

"I was not struggling," Ofelia hissed.

"I shifted and went after the mimes. They ran right after."

"They ran right after I shredded two of them into nothing," Ofelia corrected.

"Did they say anything to you?" Sully queried.

"No." Zeke shook his head. He was serious now. "They didn't say a word from what I can tell. They just attacked."

"That's how they were with me, too," Sully agreed. His gaze moved to Ofelia. "How did you know I was in trouble?"

The question caught Ofelia off guard. She knew she had to answer it, but she wasn't certain how. "Oh, well..."

"Tell me," he ordered, poking her side.

On a sigh, Ofelia rolled her neck. "I felt it."

"You felt it?" Sully had trouble wrapping his brain around that.

"I felt it," she agreed. "I was at the bar with Felix talking about couple's costume ideas and, out of the blue, I felt that you needed me. That reminds me, I should text him, so he knows I'm okay. He's probably freaking out."

"I'll stop in at Archer on my way out," Pascal countered as he stood. "I could use a drink anyway. I'll handle Felix."

Ofelia shot him a grateful look.

"I should head out too." Zeke's smile was back when he stood. "I want a drink after all this fuss."

"What about your son?" Ofelia demanded. "You're just going to pop in, shift, show me your penis, and run?"

Zeke's smile widened. "I thought I would leave the two of you to spend time together because you clearly need it. How does breakfast tomorrow sound?"

Ofelia's shoulders slumped. "Fine," she said after a beat. "It sounds fine."

"Lovely." Zeke winked at Ofelia before stopping in front of his son. "She is ... interesting."

Sully shot his father a quelling look. "She's excited. Leave her alone."

"We'll catch up tomorrow," Zeke suggested. "I'm thinking Oceana sounds good. You know it's one of my favorites."

"Fine," Sully said. "Oceana it is."

Zeke extended his hand to Ofelia. "It was a great pleasure meeting you."

Ofelia reluctantly took it. "Thanks for the assist."

"Is that what you're calling my penis?"

She made an exasperated sound deep in her throat.

"And on that note, I believe it's time to go." Zeke's smile didn't diminish as he headed out. "Have a nice night, kids."

# 4
## FOUR

Sully woke the next morning feeling rested and surprisingly warm. When he shifted, he found Ofelia had plastered herself to his back, making him the little spoon. Normally, they fell asleep with her head on his shoulder and shifted during the night, so he was the big spoon. This was a new experience.

Obviously, she'd gotten herself worked up over what had happened with the mimes the previous evening. He couldn't really blame her. If their roles had been reversed, he would've been worked up too.

If their roles had been reversed, of course, he wouldn't have been overwhelmed by a need to get to her because he had no magic to call on to fuel him. She would've been on her own.

That did not sit right with him.

"Stop thinking such deep thoughts so early in the morning," Ofelia ordered, catching him by surprise. Her voice was thick, signifying she was just waking up, and he smiled as he rolled to face her.

"How did you know I was thinking deep thoughts?" he asked as he brushed her hair away from her face. She was unbelievably beautiful—even with huge mountains of bedhead—and he was suddenly struck by the fact that if somebody told him he could never leave this bed for the rest of his life, he would be perfectly happy. When had he gotten that schmaltzy?

"I know you," Ofelia replied. She touched her finger to his cheek, tracing his laugh line. "Are you okay?"

"I actually feel pretty good. Your healing potion, per usual, is miraculous. I could do a hundred pushups and barely break a sweat at this point. I won't, mind you, because I'm warm, and you're being cuddly, but I could. I think the better question is are you okay?"

Sully watched as Ofelia's forehead creased. She seemed to be legitimately considering the question. "I don't know," she said finally. "I haven't been able to think about it much since it happened."

"Yeah." Sully rubbed his cheek against hers. "We were both caught off guard by what happened."

"It's not just that." Ofelia leaned a little closer, giving him the impression she was about to impart some great knowledge on him. "Mimes are creepy, Zach. They were pretending to be in invisible boxes. They didn't say a single word. It was just ... freaky."

Sully took a moment to absorb what she was saying, then burst out laughing. He pulled her against him, hugging her tight. "I like that you're more worked up about the fact that they were mimes than anything else."

"Well, it was creepy," Ofelia said when he pulled back to stare into her eyes. "They obviously weren't human. Or, if they were, they were enhanced by magic."

"I wish I could remember more of what happened," he

lamented. "I remember bits and pieces of it. They took me out fast."

"And yet they didn't kill you," Ofelia mused. "I wonder what they were waiting for."

Sully shot her a "are you kidding me" look. "Fe, I should think that's rather obvious. They were waiting for you to come for me. You were the target."

It was something Ofelia hadn't considered. "But..." She trailed off, clearly searching her memory. "I'm not sure what to say," she admitted after several seconds. "I guess it's possible," she hedged.

"It's not just possible. It makes the most sense. Those things aren't done by any stretch of the imagination either, so we need to be careful."

"Meaning I need to be careful," Ofelia corrected.

Sully merely shrugged. "I would prefer it if you're always careful, but that's apt enough."

Ofelia let loose a sigh. "Well, crap."

They rested together, Sully's fingers dancing up her back as he rubbed at the tension pooling there for several minutes. Then, to his surprise, she changed the subject.

"What's up with you and your father?" she asked.

Sully had been anticipating questions since he'd opened his eyes and remembered that his father had been present when he woke up on the couch the night before. He'd also managed to tick off Ofelia in record time. Her shift away from the mimes was sudden.

"My father is ... a very entitled individual," Sully replied, choosing his words carefully. "His entitlement is very different from my mother's entitlement."

"I like your mother."

"You didn't like my mother at first."

"I didn't dislike her as much as I dislike your father," Ofelia countered.

"I think you were braced to dislike my mother because you had some warning," Sully replied. "The thing with my father came out of nowhere."

"And I had to see him naked." Ofelia couldn't just let it go. "I mean ... he could've at least warned me or something."

For some reason, the fact that Ofelia was most upset about the nudity made Sully incapable of maintaining a serious demeanor.

"Have I mentioned I love you?" He snuggled her close. "Even though you have prudish sensibilities, I absolutely adore you."

Ofelia's mouth dropped open. "I do not have prudish sensibilities." She was scandalized. "He's going to be my father-in-law."

"He is," Sully readily agreed. "It's not as if he's going to be a hands-on father-in-law for you, though. I rarely see him."

"And I have questions about that."

"Of course you do." Sully flopped to his back. He wasn't in the mood for some huge, emotional discussion. Knowing Ofelia, she wasn't going to let him escape without one, though. They only had an hour and a half before they were supposed to meet Zeke for breakfast. That meant he had to get the conversation over with sooner rather than later. "Lay them on me," he prodded, resigned.

Ofelia propped herself on an elbow so she could look down at him. "Are you close with your father? Because—and I don't want to talk out of turn here—you made it sound as if you were closer to your father than your mother when she came to town."

"In some respects, I am closer to him," Sully said.

"In some respects?"

"We have that male testosterone thing going," Sully replied. He wasn't keen on having this conversation now, but he had no choice. "My mother was 'extra' when I was growing up. She always had her little tea parties going at the house. She wanted me to act a certain way, conform to a mold. My father never wanted me to fit that mold, so my relationship with him was easier."

Ofelia considered it for several seconds. "He wanted you to fit a different mold," she surmised finally.

"I didn't realize that at the time, and to be fair, the mold he wanted me to fit was the same mold he fit," Sully explained. "He didn't see it as a difficult thing to pull off."

"You did, though."

"I just wanted to be me."

"And rightfully so, because you're awesome."

Sully's lips pursed as he regarded her. She was head-strong—something he both loved and loathed at the same time—and full of herself when she was feeling ready to rumble. It was obvious that she was feeling that on his behalf right now.

"Fe, my parents didn't want anything different for me than what yours wanted for you," he argued. "They wanted me to fit in. They wanted me to be important in my community. They wanted me to succeed. Becoming a cop and moving to the French Quarter simply wasn't in their plans."

"And marrying a witch," she said. "That wasn't in their plans either."

He hated—*absolutely hated*—how conflicted she looked. "You're in my plans. That's all that matters." He was insistent as he raised his head, making sure she was looking directly into his eyes when he said the next part. "I'm living the life I want, and that includes you. Do not get weird on me."

Ofelia looked as if she was going to argue with him, then sighed. "I guess none of us ever live up to our parents' expectations," she said finally. "My mother wanted certain things for me too."

"As did your father."

"My father kind of got what he wanted," she said on a rueful smile. "Other than the fact that he's locked up in a mental health care facility right now, he pretty much got everything he wanted. Well, other than you." Now her smile turned genuine. "He wasn't looking for you to take over my life."

"Your father loves you and does the best that he can," Sully replied. "He's getting better. He's trying. I think we should give him a break."

"What about your father?" Ofelia queried. "We're meeting him for breakfast in an hour. Should we give him a break, too?"

Sully hesitated, then shook his head. "You give my father as hard of a time as you want to give him. I think he's earned it."

"You mean because he showed me his penis."

It took everything Sully had not to dissolve in laughter. "Baby, I hate to be the bearer of bad news, but we don't shift in our clothes," he said when he was reasonably assured he wouldn't set her off with his joviality. "He wasn't trying to get fresh with you."

Ofelia didn't look as if she was convinced. "We should get in the shower. I'm starving,

and we don't want to keep your father waiting."

"He's going to find something to complain about whether we keep him waiting or not."

Ofelia scowled. "You let me handle your father. If he starts complaining about you, I'm going to set his pants on fire."

Sully found he was amused at the notion. "That might make for a fun morning," he mused.

"You betcha. I'm going to rock his world."

"Then I'm really looking forward to breakfast too."


**OCEANA WAS LOCATED RIGHT OFF BOURBON** Street, which made it a regular draw for tourists. This week was light on tourists, however—it was as if they were all waiting for Halloween to show their faces and get their drink on—so there was no line out the door as was normal at Oceana when people were trying to eat their hangovers into submission.

Even though they were five minutes early, Sully wasn't surprised to find his father had already secured a table.

"Try to keep your temper in check," Sully admonished as he squeezed Ofelia's hand and led her toward his father. "If you show him that you're easily angered, he'll use that to get under your skin. Just ... let anything he says wash over you and ignore it."

Ofelia made a loud scoffing noise. "Right. That sounds just like me."

Amused yet again, Sully could do nothing but shake his head. His smile was genuine when they reached Zeke, and his father clearly took notice because Zeke was curiously allowing his gaze to bounce between them as they sat.

"You look none the worse for wear after your adventure," Zeke noted. He had a mug of coffee in front of him and appeared relaxed despite the shenanigans of the night before.

"I slept hard, and my fiancée is a master when it comes to a healing potion," Sully replied. "I feel pretty good."

"And how do you feel?" Zeke asked Ofelia. It was obviously a test, but there was nothing Sully could do to stop Ofelia from answering.

"I still feel traumatized from seeing your penis, but otherwise I'm fine," Ofelia replied. "In fact, I'm better than fine." She showed him her teeth when she smiled. "I'm on top of the world."

"What's her deal with my penis?" Zeke asked his son.

"She's only used to seeing mine," Sully replied. "Give her a break."

Ofelia made a face. "This is the French Quarter. I see random penises wherever I turn."

"She's got a point there." Sully chuckled as he moved his hand to her back. He was desperate for her to calm herself, but that didn't seem like a possibility given her current mood. "So, you're here on business?" he asked his father. He was determined to change the subject to something safer. "How long are you in town?"

Zeke held out his hands. "I have no idea. I was hoping it would be an easy deal. It doesn't look as if it's going to turn out that way, though."

"And what deal is it?" Ofelia queried. She hadn't bothered to grab a menu. She knew Oceana's menu backward and forward.

"Just a normal deal," Zeke replied. "I don't think we need to talk about business right now. Let's talk about something else. You would be bored with business talk."

"Crap," Sully muttered under his breath when Ofelia's

shoulders squared. "Why did you have to say that?" he demanded of his father.

Zeke looked confused. "That she would be bored of business talk? She will be."

"Because I'm a woman?" Ofelia demanded. She was positively furious.

"Actually, because I can't go into specific details until the deal is done—that's how real estate works, young lady —and I was trying to be polite."

Ofelia was taken aback. "Oh. I ... oh."

"Don't be mean to her," Sully warned his father. "She was just trying to get to know you outside of your penis."

"Oh, why did you have to bring it up again?" Ofelia whined. "I was just starting to forget."

Sully grinned at her and took advantage of the incoming server's presence to direct conversation to ordering for several minutes. Once the server had returned with their coffee and juice, things were calmer ... if only marginally.

"So, Zach talks about you nonstop," Zeke noted as he leaned back in his chair and regarded her. "He seems quite smitten. As I understand it, your mother is remarried to one of the gentlemen who runs the carriage tours."

"Henri Charles," Ofelia confirmed. "He's a very nice man."

"Your brother works for my son," Zeke continued.

Ofelia hesitated, unsure how to respond.

"No." Sully shook his head. Now he was the one who looked alarmed. "Felix works for himself. He's going to buy Archer from me."

Zeke's eyebrows moved toward one another. "I'm confused. I was under the impression you were becoming an entrepreneur instead of a police officer."

"Yeah, that's a big no," Sully replied. "I want to be a police officer. I'm not doing it until something better comes along. My dream is to do what I do and marry Ofelia. Felix is the one running the bar. He didn't have the capital to buy it when it was going on the market—at a steal mind you—so I essentially invested with the aim of him paying me back. It's going quite well. At this rate, he'll have me paid off in two years."

"Even with interest?" Zeke looked dubious.

"I'm not charging him interest." Sully knew it was a mistake to lay it out that way the second he said it. There was no hauling the words back into his mouth once they were out, though.

"How is that a smart move?" Zeke demanded. "That's not how business works."

Sully's frustration was palpable, and it had Ofelia shifting next to him as discomfort rolled over the table. "I am not in this for a profit," Sully snapped. "I'm in this so Felix can get a foothold in a business he's good at and not step on his sister's toes in the process."

"I'm not sure what that means." Zeke turned his gaze to Ofelia. "Would you like to explain?"

It was obvious she felt put on the spot, but she didn't stop herself from responding. "My father sold Krewe to me and left Felix out of it because he's always been a little … flaky."

"You don't have to explain anything to him," Sully growled.

"It's fine," Ofelia assured him. She meant it. She could see why Zeke had questions regarding the current arrangement. "My brother has always been unsure what he wants to do. He's very good behind a bar, though. He didn't want to lay claim to Krewe because he always thought that belonged to me. When this ... opportunity ... arose, Zach was the one who thought this plan."

"You could be making a killing," Zeke snapped at his son.

"I don't care about making a killing," Sully replied. "The bar was going to eventually go up for auction. I had a chance to get it for less than a quarter of what the bank could've gotten it for. This was not a hard decision."

"And how does that work?" Zeke demanded. "Why was it so cheap?"

"It's a long story." Sully pinched the bridge of his nose. He was suddenly tired.

"The bar previously belonged to my ex-boyfriend," Ofelia volunteered. "He was going to prison for some unfortunate life choices—he was a warlock, so it wasn't a normal prison—and Sully made a deal with him to get some immediate funds into his commissary. Sebastian agreed because he really had no other choice."

"I see." Zeke sipped his coffee before flicking his eyes back to Sully. "That's ingenious. Are there other people we can force to do that? That would be a tremendous business move."

"Of course you would think that." Sully made a face when his phone dinged with an incoming message. He was already agitated when he read it, so his mindset didn't get any better when he lowered his phone and focused on Ofelia. "Dispatch says that several bodies have been discovered in an abandoned building on Bourbon Street."

"Do you think it's a real call?" Ofelia asked.

"I would guess it is."

That wasn't good enough for Ofelia. "Do we have time to eat?"

"We have twenty minutes to eat," he said. "Then we'll

head over. It's right around the corner. I didn't say where I was, so they won't question it when I say I'm twenty minutes out."

"Why are you going with him?" Zeke asked, confused. "Do you moonlight as a cop, and I'm not aware of it?"

"Actually, sometimes I do." Ofelia shot him a toothy smile, but there was no friendliness in her eyes. "As for why I'm going, last night he got a call about a body, and he was ambushed by mimes. I'm going to make sure that doesn't happen again."

"Ah, right." Zeke bobbed his head. "I guess that makes sense."

"We'll eat fast," Sully said. "Then we'll see what's going on. It could be the real deal."

"Or it could be a trap," Ofelia said.

"Yeah. There's that possibility too."

# 5
## FIVE

Ofelia was secretly relieved when they split from Zeke after breakfast. She'd inhaled her food to the point where she choked twice and earned a healthy thump from Sully on her back to dislodge the food both times. He shot her an odd look but didn't comment. Once they'd said their goodbyes, she was more like her normal self ... although she kept muttering things under her breath that he couldn't quite make out.

"It's okay to hate my father," he said as they turned the corner onto Bourbon Street. It was still early, so there was nobody out. "There are times I hate him."

"I don't hate your father," Ofelia said automatically. She avoided making eye contact.

"Uh-huh." Sully didn't look convinced. "I'm not all that fond of your mother, for the record. It's okay not to like my father."

Ofelia opened her mouth to respond, then touched her tongue to her top lip as she changed her mind. "He seems fine," she said stiffly.

"Oh, geez." Sully made a hilarious face. "He's a jerk.

What he said about the bar deal I swung with Felix was obnoxious. He's never going to understand why I did it. That doesn't matter, though. I understand why I did it, and I'm not sorry."

Ofelia dragged her gaze back to him. "Are you sure?"

"Yeah, Fe, I'm sure. I want Felix to be established and operating on his own two feet before we have kids who are going to take the attention he's used to getting. He's a bit old to need parenting."

Ofelia murdered him with a dirty look. "He's not that bad."

"He's getting better," Sully agreed. "He's almost a full adult now. He's still got a bit of growing to do, though. I am thrilled he's no longer moonlighting as a human statue if that counts for anything."

Ofelia was sheepish. "I'm kind of glad he's over that phase too."

They walked another block before movement became obvious. Ofelia extended her hand in front of Sully, making as if she were about to shove him behind her if trouble was afoot, but he gently nudged it back. "It's my men," he assured her. "There are flashing lights down there. It's not the mimes."

"Right." Ofelia sucked in a breath. "I knew that."

Sully had to hold back a grin. "Of course you knew that. You're brilliant *and* beautiful."

"Lay off," she chided on a scowl. "I'm a bit off my game. Seeing your father's penis is still haunting me."

"Well, I can't tell you how much I love hearing you bring it up. My life gets better every single time you mention it."

That earned a giggle from Ofelia. "Sorry. I'll try to stop."

"Never stop being you." Sully gave her hand a squeeze

before moving in front of her. It was time for him to earn his paycheck and exert control over the scene. "Detective Sully." He flashed his badge for the approaching uniform. "I got a call that you found some bodies?"

"Officer Crooks, Sir," the uniform replied, bobbing his chin. "We *did* find bodies. There are three of them. Up there." He pointed toward the second-floor window of the building they were in front of.

"Is there an apartment up there?" Ofelia queried.

Crooks shot her a dubious look. "Ma'am, this is no place for civilians."

Ofelia shot Sully a death glare. "Unbelievable," she muttered under her breath.

Sully kept his face impassive. "Ms. Archer works as a consultant for the department," he said forcefully. "She's here to help because she's a business owner and is familiar with the businesses on this stretch of Bourbon Street." It was a lie, but it wasn't out of the realm of possibility. "Right?" he prodded her.

Ofelia wasn't keen on justifying her presence, but she nodded all the same. "Right. This was Cajun Cocktails up until about two months ago. It went under before the end of the season."

"I can't picture that bar," Sully admitted.

"That's because it wasn't here very long. It was one of the ones that opens after the first of the year and closes before the next year. You have to hit your gimmick right if you expect to keep business going on Bourbon Street for multiple seasons."

"Do you know who owns the building?" Sully queried.

Here Ofelia hesitated. "I'm not sure," she hedged. "I think—stress *think*—that this is one of the buildings that went to the bank after Katrina."

"The bank kept a building for twenty years?" Sully asked dumbly. "That doesn't sound right."

"It happened with some of the more desirable buildings," Ofelia explained. "The bank people knew that there would always be something new going into this particular building. Therefore, it made good financial sense to hold onto it."

"There's obviously no one in there now," Crooks argued.

"That's because the business owner went out of business," Ofelia replied. "He would've come in with an offer to the bank late last year. Then he would've opened the new business sometime after Christmas. He probably had a good Mardi Gras and assumed everything was going to be okay."

"Because all the bars are packed to the seams during Mardi Gras," Sully said.

Ofelia nodded. "Once Mardi Gras was over, reality would've set in. Cajun Cocktails was not a good gimmick. There's a reason the Bourbon Street bars that sustain hang on. They market themselves perfectly. The rent here is exorbitant, so once the Mardi Gras high dissipated, they would've been running on fumes until folding. Now the bank will start all over again. A new tenant will come in before the end of the year and the cycle will repeat."

"What happens if they find a bar that sticks?" Sully queried.

"Then everybody is happy, including the bank." Ofelia's eyes moved to the second-floor window. She could see movement through the glass. "Is that apartment being rented out? I don't know a lot of the business owners—and that includes the banks—renting out the apartments now. They tend to be keeping them for offices instead."

"Nobody is living there, ma'am," Crooks replied.

Ofelia scowled. "Don't call me ma'am."

Crooks pretended he hadn't heard her. "There are people living in the unit next door. You can't access the space without going downstairs and then back up again, though."

"I hate it when people call me ma'am," Ofelia complained to Sully.

He absently patted her shoulder. She clearly wasn't having a good day. "I'm sorry, ma'am."

Ofelia practically skinned him with a single look. "What about the dead people?" she demanded. "Do you know who they are?"

"No identification has been made at this time," Crooks replied. It was almost as if he was getting bored with the conversation. "We were waiting for Detective Sully to arrive on the scene."

"Then take me to the bodies," Sully said.

Crooks nodded and motioned for them to follow him. He took them around the side of the building and pointed toward a stairwell. "Go up there. It's hard to miss them once you're on the second floor." His gaze moved to Ofelia. "It's a bad scene, ma'am."

"I'm sure I've seen worse," Ofelia replied. "Also, if you call me ma'am again, I'm going to castrate you. You've been warned." She stomped toward the steps, leaving Sully to meet the uniform's questioning gaze.

"Call her Ms. Archer if you want to keep your manhood. If you're not comfortable with that, or can't remember, then refrain from calling her anything. She's serious about the 'ma'am' stuff. She hates it."

"And you know that how?" Crooks challenged. "I thought she was just a consultant."

Sully wasn't about to fall for the trap. It wasn't as if Crooks was being clever. "She's more than one thing to me. That's how she got the job. That doesn't mean her wishes shouldn't be respected. Don't call her ma'am, okay? It's not that hard."

Crooks let loose a long-suffering sigh. "Of course, sir."

Sully left the man to wallow—and likely speculate— and headed up after Ofelia. He could hear voices as he approached the second floor, and when he slid inside the nearest unit through the open door, he wasn't surprised to find two uniforms talking to Ofelia. What he was surprised to find were three bodies arranged in the middle of the room. They almost looked as if they were part of an art installation. Their feet pointed toward one another, and their heads flowed outward.

"Detective Sully." He held up his badge, his gaze never leaving the bodies. "What in the hell happened here?"

"Officer Parker," one of the uniforms replied, introducing himself. "As for what happened, we're honestly not sure. They were clearly stabbed—"

"The knives sticking out of their chests are a dead giveaway for that," Sully agreed.

"But we're not certain why they were posed this way," Parker continued. "It clearly happened after death."

"What tipped you guys off to check this building?" Sully asked.

"One of the business owners across the street called last night," Parker replied. "He thought there were squatters in here and suggested we roust them. It didn't seem like an immediate threat, so it was prioritized low. We made our way around to do it today and obviously it should've been prioritized higher."

"You couldn't have known." Sully cocked his head as he

regarded the bodies. "Have you checked them for identification?"

"No, sir." Parker shook his head. "We've been waiting for you."

"Right." Sully took a pair of rubber gloves from Parker and dropped down next to the nearest body. He stared hard at the man's face—they were all men, two black and one white—and then started digging around in his pockets looking for a wallet.

"You're not going to find anything," Ofelia noted. She'd moved over to a different body and dropped down. She wasn't wearing gloves, so she couldn't touch anything, but it wasn't necessary. "I know these guys."

Sully's eyebrows moved toward his hairline. "Meaning what?"

"Meaning that I've seen them before." Ofelia was grim as she tentatively reached out to touch the arm of the nearest man. She'd forgotten she wasn't alone with Sully, and that wasn't allowed.

"Ma'am, no." Parker vehemently shook his head as he stopped her.

"Geez." Ofelia snatched her hand back and glared at him. "What is it with you guys calling me ma'am?" She was beside herself.

"It's a term of respect, ma'am," Parker replied. He looked annoyed.

"Give her some gloves," Sully ordered. "As for you, pay attention to me." He was firm as he drew Ofelia's gaze to him. "Where do you know these guys from?"

"They bed down on the benches outside Jackson Square at night," Ofelia replied as she accepted the gloves from Parker. She wasn't certain she could use her magic while wearing them, but she didn't have much of a choice. "They're regulars."

Sully nodded. He'd been afraid of that. At least two of the men looked vaguely familiar to him too. "Do you know their names?"

"Just their street names." Ofelia snapped the gloves into place with a flourish and pointed. "That's Roman. He fancied himself a gladiator and rushed to the rescue of any woman he saw getting sexually harassed."

"He must have been busy in the Quarter," Parker mused. "Sexual harassment and alcohol go together hand in hand."

"His favorite stomping ground was the steps in front of the Supreme Court building," Ofelia continued. "He made the whole circuit of that area, from Royal House down past Mr. B's and then he would circle back in front of Hotel Monteleone before landing on the steps again for a rest."

"How do you know that?" Parker asked. He looked suddenly suspicious. "Were you involved with this guy?"

Ofelia's glare was withering. "When you spend time not ignoring the regulars, you learn their routines," she fired back. "I've spent my fair share of time trying to help people in Jackson Square. Give me a break."

"Definitely give her a break," Sully agreed. "She's my fiancée."

"I thought she was a consultant," Parker shot back. "That's what they're saying down on the street. They radioed up when you were coming."

"She *is* a consultant. She's also my fiancée. In fact..." Sully trailed off. He was about to lose his temper, and it was a waste of time. "You know what? You guys can head down to the street level. We'll take it from here." His tone was icy and firm. There was no pushing back on it.

"Sir?" Parker was obviously confused.

"You heard me." Sully turned his back on the officer. "I don't need your disrespect today. Three people are dead. I want to hear from the person who is actually giving me actionable information."

Parker worked his jaw, and Sully had the distinct impression that he was going to say something snarky. Instead, he snapped his jaw shut and stomped out of the room. The other officer followed him. Sully waited until he'd heard the door that led to the stairwell slam shut to speak.

"I'm going to have to file a report about that," he lamented. "I hate paperwork."

Ofelia took the opportunity to remove her gloves without asking. She knew Sully wouldn't give her grief for touching the bodies. "You could've just ignored him," she noted as she touched her fingertip to Roman's wrist. After a few seconds, she shook her head and tried the next body. "Nothing," she said after several seconds. "I can't pick up anything from them."

"Do you think that's deliberate? Like ... could someone be trying to stop you from seeing what happened to them?"

"You mean the mimes?"

Sully lifted one shoulder. "It's possible, right?"

"It is," she agreed. "I don't think we should land on it being probable, though. Right now, we have no reason to assume it's the mimes. They were interested in us, not random homeless people."

"You have a point." Sully moved to the next body and checked for identification. "None of these guys are going to have wallets." He already knew that was true, and yet he checked the third body anyway. "It's going to be hard to identify them off street names. One or two of them might have arrests in their pasts and fingerprints on file, but I doubt we'll identify all three of them that way."

"Cobra over there was local," Ofelia offered, tilting her chin toward the body closest to Sully. "I know because I was getting an iced tea at Jackson Square when his niece came across him. She was from Bywater. I heard her talking to him. She was trying to get him to come home. The way she made it sound, they take turns coming over at regular intervals to try to talk him into going home.

"She saw me staring at her when she was leaving and explained they know he's not going home, but they feel they need to try, and they're always going to be there if he's ready," she continued. "I think they hoped he would have a 'come to Jesus' moment."

"Maybe he did at the end," Sully said.

"Maybe." Ofelia flashed a tight smile. "I'm betting his real identity is going to be the easiest to track down. As for this one, I only saw him a handful of times." She pointed toward the third dead body. "I believe they called him Godzilla because he would start roaring in the middle of a conversation if it went in a direction he wasn't comfortable with."

"Mental illness?" Sully queried.

"They all have a form of mental illness," Ofelia replied. "His was pretty serious, though. I never saw him hanging out with anybody. He was always on the fringe of the other groups. Cobra was popular. He would entertain people around Jackson Square. Roman was friendly enough too. This guy, though, I remember thinking that he was likely a bomb that was set to go off."

Sully blew out a sigh. "I think that can be said for a lot of them. It's entirely possible he was arrested before, though. If he had issues like that, it's likely someone called the cops on him."

"Yeah." Ofelia turned her attention away from the faces and focused on the knives. "These are all ritual daggers. They're not exactly the same, but I'm willing to bet they were purchased at area voodoo stores."

"I would say you're right," Sully agreed. He angled his head to get a better look. "I bet these knives didn't cost more than twenty bucks each."

"They're not expensive, so the clerk who sold them might not remember who bought them. It wouldn't have stuck out."

"We don't even know if they were purchased from the same store," Sully pointed out. "For all we know, they're part of someone's collection."

"It has to be more than one person," Ofelia pressed. "I mean ... sure, they were all mentally ill in their own right, but one person couldn't have controlled all three of them." She looked around. "Do you see any empty bottles?"

It took Sully a moment to realize what she was getting at. "Oh." He pursed his lips and looked in each corner. "No. No bottles. No drugs that I see."

"Maybe they weren't even killed here," Ofelia mused. "There's not a lot of blood."

"Maybe that's because they died before they were stabbed."

It was something Ofelia hadn't considered, but it made sense. "Huh." She rested the back of her hand against Roman's forehead. "Their bodies are cold. They've been dead for hours."

"Oh, most definitely," Sully agreed. "They died yesterday. I'm curious to know if they died before or after our incident on Royal Street."

"Only the coroner can answer that question, right?"

"Pretty much." Sully pulled his phone out of his pocket. "I'm going to see what's taking the coroner so long. If you need to touch anything, make sure to wipe your finger-prints afterward. I don't want to give Officer Parker a reason to get us in trouble. I'm sure he's going to file a report of his own."

Ofelia found it difficult to hide her worry on the subject. She smiled all the same. "I know the drill. I just don't think there's anything here to find."

"That means there's a secondary site. We need to find where it is."

That was easier said than done, but Ofelia didn't disagree with him. "Yeah. There definitely has to be a secondary site or some magical element we're missing. We need to find out which one it is ... and fast."

# 6

## SIX

S ully gave Parker a dirty look as he and Ofelia exited the building twenty minutes later. They'd searched everywhere and come up missing.

"Have you canvassed the neighborhood?" he asked Crooks, who either didn't realize something had happened between Parker and Sully or didn't care.

"We have, but these apartments aren't full. There is one woman who lives in that building." Crooks pointed. "She's over there right now holding court."

Ofelia followed his finger with her eyes and had to bite back a smile when she saw an older woman—she had to be pushing eighty—putting on a show for several curious onlookers. She used big hand gestures and appeared to be enjoying her moment in the sun.

"Did she say anything good?" Sully queried.

Crooks lifted one shoulder in a shrug. "I don't know. It depends on who you ask. I happen to think she's full of it. You might think differently. Her name is Ruby Christopher, in case you're interested."

Sully motioned for Ofelia to follow him as he

approached the woman. He looked leery but resigned. "Ruby?" he prodded when they were close.

The woman jerked her eyes in their direction. She looked to be midstory and annoyed about being interrupted. "Who are you?" she demanded after several seconds.

Sully held up his badge. "Detective Sully." He returned the badge to his pocket. "Do you have a few minutes?"

"I already told my story to those other cops." Ruby patted her gray hair, which was pulled back in a loose bun. "Why do you need to hear it again?"

"Because I'm the one in charge, and I like hearing things for myself," Sully replied calmly. "I won't keep you but a minute."

Ruby eyed him for a beat longer and then looked at Ofelia. "You're Oscar's daughter," she said out of the blue.

Ofelia nodded. "I am. Do you know my father?"

"I know that he's gone." Ruby looked momentarily sad as she let Sully lead her away from the people she'd been entertaining. "Did you bury him?"

Ofelia did her best to pretend the question didn't bother her. "He's not dead. He's just away for a little bit."

"Oh, to the nut farm?" Ruby nodded. "I heard that story too. I didn't think it was really true, though. He said he would die before he'd end up in one of those places."

Ofelia had to bite the inside of her cheek to keep from exploding. Oscar's meltdowns had become the stuff of legend in the French Quarter. Everybody knew he struggled at times.

Sully shot her a quelling look before drawing Ruby's attention to him. "Did you see something happening in the building next door last night?"

Ruby nodded solemnly. "It was a satanic ritual."

"You saw them performing a satanic ritual?" Sully was understandably dubious. "How so?"

"I saw shadows. They were dancing in tandem. I heard chanting."

Ofelia darted a look toward Sully but didn't say anything.

"You heard chanting?" Sully waited for her to nod. "Okay, well, did you see anything?"

"I saw clowns, and they were smiling." Ruby no longer looked as if she was enjoying herself. "I peeked through the windows. If I look at the right angle, I can see through to the second floor. It was a lot more fun when the pervert had an office up there and banged drunks for free drinks. Last night ... last night was different."

Sully's expression was hard to read. "How was it different?"

"They had three people with them. Three people who weren't clowns. They weren't there, though. They were ... it was like they were under a spell."

Ofelia's senses tingled, but she struggled overtime to keep her expression neutral. "How so?"

"They floated around with the clowns. They had these huge smiles on their faces. They were drugged or something ... or under hypnosis. I don't know. It was as if they were in that movie."

"What movie?" Sully queried.

"She must be talking about the Joker in *Batman*," Ofelia replied.

Ruby pinned Ofelia with a withering look. "No, I wasn't talking about the Joker. I was talking about that horror movie. The one where everybody smiles real big and then the person seeing the smiles dies with a big old smile on their face."

Ofelia had to take a moment to figure out what was being said. Then she nodded. "*Smile.* The movie with Kevin Bacon's daughter. I saw that with Felix last Halloween. They were showing it at this outdoor party on one of those big screens. It was creepy."

"And you think we're dealing with the movie *Smile*?" Sully queried.

"No." Ofelia shook her head. "Definitely not. I'm just finally understanding what she's talking about."

"It was a satanic ritual," Ruby whispered. "We're all doomed."

"Yeah, I think we're going to want to get you a room next to Oscar in the nut farm if you keep saying stuff like that," Sully drawled.

Ruby scowled at him. "You're the one who asked."

"Yes. I'm kind of sorry I did." Sully talked to Ruby for another few minutes before cutting her loose. Then he moved with Ofelia to the sidewalk so they could talk away from prying ears. "I'm pretty sure the clowns she was referring to were the mimes."

Ofelia nodded. "Yeah. That would be my guess too."

"Where do you think we should go to next to get answers? I mean ... who else might have seen the mimes last night and not assumed they were drunks running around and looking for attention?"

Ofelia only had one answer. "I think it's time for you to buy me an iced tea in Jackson Square."

"Right." Sully rolled his neck. "I guess that's our only option, isn't it?"

"I don't know about only, but it seems to be our best option."

"Then let's head out."

"I'm right behind you."

· · ·

**THE SKY WAS OVERCAST, BUT THERE WAS** no rain falling when they arrived in Jackson Square. Like Bourbon Street the night before, the crowd was sparse.

"Is it wrong that I'm glad to have a bit of a break before the Halloween rush?" Ofelia asked as they cut in front of St. Louis Cathedral.

"Actually, I'm all for a break," Sully replied. "We could both use it."

"Have you thought of a Halloween costume yet?"

"I have." Sully was solemn when he nodded, making Ofelia suspicious.

"And what is it?" Ofelia queried.

"Han and Leia."

Ofelia's first instinct was to kill the suggestion. Instead, she thought about it. "Huh."

"I was going to go with Luke and Leia because he has the cool lightsaber—"

"And you like the idea of carrying around a magic stick," Ofelia surmised.

"Right you are." He winked at her. "I don't want people giving me grief for making out with you if I'm dressed as Luke, though. Incest jokes are never funny."

"Yes, you don't want to be looking for love in Alderaan places," Ofelia agreed.

Sully almost tripped when he got the joke. "That was terrible," he said on a laugh, earning a smile from her.

"I am a funny girl," she said. Her eyes landed on a familiar face when she began scanning. "I didn't know he was spending his days out here again," she said as she inclined her head toward one of the homeless ambassadors.

Bernie Portman was close with both Ofelia and Sully.

Recently, he'd been living in Ofelia's new building—which was undergoing renovations—and serving as a guard of sorts. He preferred the privacy, even though the building was loud and full of dust. Ofelia hadn't seen him in days, though.

"I think he comes out here during the day," Sully replied. "He doesn't want to grow too far removed from the community. He still beds down in the other building at night."

Ofelia didn't know if she believed that. "We need to check on him more often. I don't want him feeling lonely."

"I don't want him feeling lonely either," Sully agreed. "The problem is that he chafes if we actively parent him too much."

"Oh, don't call me a mommy."

Sully smirked. "He's an adult and doesn't want us watching over his shoulder. I don't know what to tell you."

Ofelia made a face, then she recovered. "Let's go talk to him now. If anybody has heard the skinny on our dead guys, it's likely him."

"Probably," Sully agreed. "Don't push him too hard about having a curfew or anything, though. You're going to push him right out the door if you're not careful."

"I'm not going to push him. Why do you think I'm going to push him?"

"You are Marie Charles's daughter."

Ofelia's mouth fell open. "That could be the most horrible thing you've ever said to me."

"I still love you." He shot her a teasing wink before sliding over to Bernie. The older man was seemingly caught up in the conversation he was having with two of the regular faces that hung around Jackson Square. When he looked over, he didn't appear happy to find Sully moving in on him.

"Oh, don't tell me something terrible happened," Bernie complained.

"That's not an option." Sully managed a wan smile. "We just came from Bourbon Street. Three of your friends —or your acquaintances I guess—are dead. We found them in an apartment over one of the vacant bar fronts."

Bernie gripped the cane he was holding tighter. He'd taken to bringing it with him wherever he went, even though he swore up and down he didn't need it. That told Ofelia that he was feeling the arthritis she knew was plaguing him more and more. She would have to come up with a potion to help him. She refused to let him suffer. Now wasn't the time to bring that up, however. They had bigger worries.

"Who?" Bernie asked.

Sully darted a look toward Ofelia.

"Cobra for one," Ofelia replied. "I know he was local. Do you guys know how to find his family? We don't have a real name for him."

"I'm not sure if I ever heard a real name for him," Bernie replied. "I can ask around, though. You said there were three of them. Who else?"

Ofelia's stomach constricted as she prepared to deliver the bad news. "Godzilla."

Bernie was rueful. "That's sad, but I'm surprised he lasted as long as he did. He was not all there." He gestured toward his head and twirled a finger.

"It was Roman, too, Bernie." Ofelia's voice was soft, and her heart threatened to shred when Bernie's face contorted.

"No." Bernie vehemently shook his head. "I just saw Roman. He was doing his regular circuit on Royal yesterday.

They've even started giving him glasses of water when he passes Hotel Monteleone. He keeps the unsavory element away, and they like him."

"If they like him so much, they could give him more than water," one of the men Bernie had been talking with said. "I mean ... there's a bar right there on the other side of the door. It moves and everything."

Even though it was a sad conversation, Sully smiled. "I agree. He deserved way more than water."

"He's not really gone, is he?" Bernie asked in a raspy voice. "He was one of the good ones."

"I'm sorry, but he is gone," Ofelia replied. "I recognized him right away when I saw the bodies."

"Where were they?" Bernie asked.

"On Bourbon Street. You know that place that used to be Cajun Cocktails? They were found in the apartment on the second floor."

"Huh." Bernie chewed on his bottom lip. "Did they go there for a specific reason? I mean ... I didn't know any of them to want to hang out on Bourbon Street. That wasn't the scene any of them appreciated."

"We don't think they were killed where they were found," Sully replied. "At least ... we're having trouble wrapping our heads around what happened."

"And what did happen?" one of the other men queried. Ofelia was fairly certain his name was Pike. He hadn't spoken since their arrival but looked invested now.

"Right now, the only thing we know is that they were found on the floor, and their bodies had been arranged."

Bernie snapped up his chin. "Arranged how?"

"Like a pinwheel," Sully replied. "Their feet were all pointing at one another, and they were spread out at even intervals. They all had knives protruding from their chests."

"The knives were just left there?" Pike didn't look impressed. "Why waste a knife like that?"

"We don't know." Sully held out his hands. He was genuinely at a loss. "The thing is, there wasn't much blood up there. Certainly not enough to legitimize three stab wounds."

"What does that mean?" Bernie queried.

"It means that the knives could've been inserted into the chests after they were already dead. It means the bodies could've been exsanguinated somehow. It means that something else we can't even fathom happened."

Bernie snapped his gaze to Ofelia. "What do you think? You're the expert on stuff like this."

"I think that they were likely killed some other way, and the knives were left behind as some sort of message," she replied.

"What kind of message?"

"That we don't know."

"We're going to figure it out, though," Sully added. "I promise."

"What do you want from us?" Pike asked.

"Well, for starters, when was the last time you saw the three of them?" Sully took the notebook out of his pocket so he could jot down some quick notes. "Did they ever hang out together?"

"They might've hung out together like I'm hanging with those guys over there," Bernie replied, gesturing toward three other individuals who regularly bedded down in Jackson Square at night. "They weren't friendly, though. They didn't hate each other or nothing, but they weren't friendly either."

"Godzilla wasn't friendly with anybody," Pike added. "He just liked wandering around and roaring."

"That is ... unfortunate," Sully said. "What about Roman and Cobra?"

"Roman had a regular route he walked every single day," Bernie replied. "I saw him doing it yesterday. At the time, nothing was wrong. I even stopped to talk to him."

"What did you say?" Ofelia queried.

"I just told him to beware of the mimes. Apparently, they're everywhere ... and they're acting weird."

Ofelia rested her hand on the back of the nearest bench and sucked in a breath. "Mimes?" she managed to squeak out.

Bernie shot her an odd look out of the corner of his eye. "Have you seen them?"

"We had occasion to run into them on Royal Street last night," Sully replied. "They took off."

"Royal Street?" Bernie arched an eyebrow. "The same Royal Street where Roman regularly hung out? Was he with them?"

"He definitely wasn't with them," Ofelia replied. "There was a group of them, but they didn't have anybody I recognized with them."

"What were they doing?"

"What have you seen them doing?" Sully interjected. "We didn't get to see much of them last night. They were just ... odd."

*They were more than odd,* Ofelia internally mused. It wasn't a story they could share, though. Not when it involved a naked panther shifter and a vampire scaling tall buildings with a single bound while carrying her fiancé as if he weighed no more than a school backpack.

"They've just been hanging around," Pike replied.

"When did you first see them?" Sully prodded. "Like ... have they been here for days or weeks?"

"I'm not sure." Pike darted a questioning look toward Bernie. "I guess it was about a week and a half ago?"

Bernie put a thumb up in agreement. "That sounds about right. Ten days ago or so, Smoky said that there were clowns dancing on the riverwalk. He said it was creepy. We went to take a look and realized it wasn't clowns— although we all agreed mimes were just as bad as clowns— and we watched them for a little bit."

"How many of them were there?"

"That first night there were three of them," Bernie replied. "They just stood out there, pretending to juggle and stuff. They did this weird thing where they pretended to be in an invisible box."

"I'm familiar with what mimes do," Sully said, his distaste evident. "I don't need a rehash of that stuff. Just tell us whatever you can about what the mimes have been doing over the past few days."

"That's just it." Bernie held out the hand not gripping the cane. "They've been seen multiple times. They're normally out on the riverwalk, but they've been seen on Bourbon Street and even dancing around the Square after dark."

"Are there multiple groups, or do they only show up as one group?"

"I have no idea. I just know I've never seen one of them alone. There're at least three of them together, and I've seen as many as six of them hanging out on the riverwalk."

"Are they only out after dark?"

"I've never seen them during the day. Dusk and after."

Sully nodded. "So, they travel in packs and only come out after dark."

"We don't know that they only come out after dark," Ofelia argued. "We just know that these guys haven't seen them during the day. They sleep late, though. They tend to be out late."

"She's not wrong," Bernie agreed. "It's possible they're out during the day."

Sully tilted his head, considering, then held out his hand for Ofelia. "Let's take a walk, huh?"

Ofelia slipped her hand into his and nodded. "It can't possibly hurt." She smiled at the others before they left. "Thanks for the information."

"What are you going to do when you find them?" Pike queried. "Will you kill them?"

"That's certainly a possibility," Sully replied. "We'll have to wait and see. For now, just be careful and stay away from the mimes."

"You don't have to tell us twice," Bernie assured him. "Mimes are creepy."

"They certainly are."

# 7
## SEVEN

The riverwalk was busy enough, but it was locals exercising and hanging out instead of the normal tourist traffic. Sully and Ofelia walked half a mile in each direction before turning around. Walking aimlessly and burning time was going to get them nowhere.

"We have to wait until we're certain they're out," Sully said as they headed toward the stairs that led back to Jackson Square. "I'll send out an edict that all reports of mimes are sent to me. And how freaky is that? I'm hunting mimes."

"Not alone you're not," Ofelia warned. Her eyes were dark. "You'd better not even consider doing anything yourself with those mimes. It won't end well."

"I've got it." Sully managed a smile for her benefit before nipping in for a kiss. "You're very forceful when you're feeling protective."

"Try scared," Ofelia countered. "Last night, when I got the feeling that you were in trouble, it almost knocked me off my stool. I thought I was going to be sick."

"I'm fine," he reminded her, tapping his chest. "I'm right in front of you, and I'm fine."

Ofelia gave him a dirty look. "None of this feels fine."

"Well, we have to play the hand we're dealt." Sully was matter of fact. "You got to me. I'm good. Now we have to focus on going after the mimes, not what almost happened."

Ofelia's lower lip came out to play. "You're basically saying I'm whiny."

He chuckled. "Not in general. Most of the time you're an absolute delight. Occasionally, you turn whiny, though. Fear does it to you most of the time. Fear for Felix. Fear for your father. Now fear for me. You can't change what happened though."

"I guess I'm still a little haunted by it," Ofelia acknowledged. "I don't mean to be such a pill."

"I know." Sully gave her rear end a friendly pat. "We need to move past it, though."

"I think it was compounded by the fact that I saw your father's penis."

"What did I say?" Sully's eyes flashed with annoyance. "Stop saying that. It sounds dirty."

This time it was Ofelia's turn to smile. "Sorry." She held up her hands in placating fashion. "I didn't mean to upset you."

"Lies." Sully made a clucking sound with his tongue as he shook his head. "You like getting me riled up." He lightly smacked her rear end for good measure. "Ignore my father. He's out of our lives for now."

To Ofelia, that was a weird declaration. There was no point in arguing about it now, however. "What's our next step?"

"I have to go to the coroner's office."

Ofelia stilled. "Have you been there since..." She trailed off.

"Since we found the mole and put them through the wringer with an investigation? I have not. It will be an adventure."

"Do you want me to come with you?"

The question tickled Sully. "More than anything. It can't happen, though. It's one thing to bring you in as a consultant on the street. The uniforms would have to go through my boss to question your presence."

"I guarantee Parker is doing just that today," Ofelia said dryly.

"Maybe so, but the higher-ups will understand exactly why I wanted you with me."

"Because I'm cute?'

Sully's lips quirked. "The cutest," he readily agreed. "I still can't take you with me to the coroner's office. It will end badly."

On a sigh, Ofelia nodded. "Fine. What are you going to do after that?"

"I'm not sure. If we can identify these guys, I would like to talk to their families. That might take longer than a few hours, though."

"Right." Ofelia danced her fingers over Sully's chest, causing him to catch her hand.

"No finger wandering," he warned. "We're on a very serious mission. If you keep doing that, I'm going to have to find us a hotel room ... and the ones that rent by the hour aren't up to your standards."

That elicited a chuckle from Ofelia. "The ones that rent by the hour aren't in the French Quarter at all."

"True." He leaned in and gave her a quick kiss before taking a step back. "What are you going to do?"

"I'm going to stop in and see Pascal. I want to thank him for last night and see if he knows anything about the mimes. We didn't really get a chance to talk."

"Because you were so worked up."

"Because your father surprised me," Ofelia countered. "I don't get worked up."

"Right." Sully's chuckle was light. "Not my Fe." He sobered after a few seconds. "I think seeing Pascal is a good idea. We'll touch base after I talk to the coroner. Are you going to Krewe when you're finished with Pascal?"

"For now," Ofelia confirmed. "I can't guarantee I won't make a run elsewhere, but for now that's the plan." She was quiet a beat. "I'll probably stop in and see my dad on the way back from Pascal's place, before I head to Krewe."

Sully was caught off guard. "I thought we weren't scheduled to see him until tomorrow."

"We're not but..." Ofelia paused, uncertain how she wanted to proceed. Ultimately, she sighed. "The vampires taunted him because he was my father. If the mimes really are after me—or even just after you—then he could be a target. I want to make sure he hasn't been seeing them."

Realization dawned on Sully, and he nodded. "That makes sense. I think that's a good idea. I can try to hurry and meet you there."

"That's not necessary," Ofelia assured him. "I'll be okay. Dad has been better."

Oscar *had* been better the last several visits. Sully was afraid that Ofelia would be crushed when her father ultimately had a setback, however. And Oscar would eventually have a setback. He just hoped it wasn't today.

"Okay, well, keep in touch. I'll do the same. We'll reconvene by dinner at the very least."

"That sounds good." Ofelia's smile was bright. "Just one thing."

"Oh, I'm going to hate this, aren't I? That's why you're saving it for last."

"I have no idea." Ofelia shrugged. "I'm just curious what we're going to do with your father."

"Like ... you want to know if we're going to have to hide his body in one of the mausoleums?"

The look Ofelia shot him was withering. "No. That's not what I was talking about. I want to know when we're going to see him again."

"Oh." Sully wasn't certain how to respond. "I'm sure if he wants to see me, he'll call."

That wasn't the answer Ofelia was expecting. "That's it? You're not going to go out of your way to see him?"

"No. We're not really that close."

"But—"

"It's not like it is with your family," Sully insisted. "We're not all up in each other's business. It's fine."

Ofelia was certain there was an insult buried in there, but she didn't comment on it. There was no reason. "Fine. We'll fight about your father later. We don't need to do it now."

"See, I like how you're thinking."

"You would."

OFELIA WENT STRAIGHT TO PASCAL'S STORE upon separating from Sully. She found the taciturn vampire in his usual spot—on his velvet throne—in the middle of his store when she entered. He didn't bother to look up from the huge book he was reading.

Ofelia knew that he wasn't really interested in the book.

For all she—and likely he—knew, the book was an old encyclopedia or something, not the magical tome he presented it to be. His interest was purely for the magazine tucked away inside of the book. It was either *In Touch*, *People*, or another magazine of that ilk because the only thing Pascal enjoyed reading was gossip rags.

He didn't even check who had entered his store before he started ranting. "They're saying that Britney Spears's ex-husband might be moving to Hawaii just to force her to pay more child support. I mean ... get a job, dude. Why does she have to pay for all those other kids?" He lifted his eyes to her. "What do you think?"

Ofelia took a moment to consider the question. "I think that two things can be true at once. I think that maybe Britney might need some meds and also, her ex-husband should get a job and stop trying to live on her dime."

"I can see that." Pascal closed the book and focused on her. "How are you after last night?"

The question wasn't easy to answer. Instead of immediately responding in a specific way, she flopped down in the chair across from him and really considered her answer. "I don't like Zach's dad." It was something she wouldn't admit in front of anyone other than Pascal or Felix. She would be too afraid of it getting back to Sully to ever say it to somebody else.

"I don't think Sully likes his dad, so I don't know why you're fretting about it."

"Yeah, but he has a reason to dislike his father—they have history—and I'm just basing my opinion on twenty minutes of banter, one penis flash, and a very uncomfortable breakfast. Shouldn't I be trying to get along with his father for his sake?"

"No."

"How can you be so flippant?"

"Because I've known Topher for a very long time and, quite frankly, he sucks as a person. If he were in one of my magazines, he would be a Kardashian ... and not one of the good ones."

Ofelia was amused despite herself. "I didn't realize there were good Kardashians."

"It's a sliding scale. He would also be right up there with the guy who cheated on his girlfriend on *Vanderpump Rules*. He's a tool."

Ofelia had never known Pascal to be so matter of fact about someone. He usually talked about people in gray terms. He was definitely living in a black and white world today. "Sully goes out of his way to deal with my mother, though," she pointed out. "She's kind of a tool, too. I feel I should be a better fiancée."

"Aw." Pascal mock-clutched at his heart. "That's truly touching."

Ofelia glowered at him. "I don't appreciate you mocking me."

"And I don't appreciate you being so ridiculous." Pascal dropped his hands. "Ofelia, Sully loves you. I wasn't certain he was a good match at first because I knew his father. It turns out that he's your best match ... and that's because he's nothing like his father. I don't think he expects you to like Topher."

"Yeah." Ofelia pressed her lips together as she thought about it. "How is Zeke a nickname for Topher in the first place?" she asked out of nowhere. "I mean ... that's just stupid. It makes no sense. I can see if his nickname was Goober or something. That's something a parent would call a kid. Zeke is another name, though."

"Yes, I too am traumatized thinking about how that

happened," Pascal agreed. "Is that why you're here? If you're going to start ranting, I'm prepared to force myself to make sympathetic noises as I read. I won't really be listening, but I can pretend."

Ofelia glared at him. "No. I'm not here because of the nickname. I'm here because three bodies were found down on Bourbon Street this morning."

Pascal straightened. "Anyone we know?"

Ofelia caught him up, leaving nothing out. When she got to the part about the mimes, he muttered something she couldn't quite make out under his breath. He was solemn as she finished.

"I've heard about the mimes," Pascal volunteered. "I've heard three stories now. I haven't managed to see them in person yet, though. That's why I went running when I heard they were out last night."

"They have to want something," Ofelia insisted.

"Oh, I'm certain they want something very specific," Pascal agreed. "Unfortunately, I don't know what that something is. We need to figure it out, though ... and sooner rather than later. Otherwise, I think we're all going to suffer."

Ofelia was right there with him.


**SULLY WAS NERVOUS WHEN ENTERING THE** coroner's office. He'd been doing his job when he found the mole covering up for a pack of local vampires who were killing people and then hiding the paperwork when the bodies came through the morgue. Two people had been caught— one right away and one more than a week after—and they'd been arrested. People in the department had been walking on eggshells since.

Deep down, Sully didn't feel guilty. He was sorry those who were innocent had been dragged into this. The department had to be cleaned up for things to keep running smoothly, however. He couldn't be sorry about cleaning things up.

"Hey." Pansy Smith was at the front desk when he approached. She was young, blonde, and full of energy. She'd been flirting with Sully for two straight years, constantly dropping hints about where she would be in case he "accidentally" crossed paths with her. Her smile was at the ready when she saw it was him, so obviously, she wasn't holding anything against him.

"Hey." Sully returned her smile. "I need to see whoever is handling the bodies discovered on Bourbon Street this morning."

"That would be Dr. Caldwell," Pansy offered. "He's in with the bodies now. Third door on the left down that hall." She pointed.

"Thank you." Sully moved to step in that direction, but Pansy stopped him with a nervous laugh.

"It's sad about those people dying, but we're going down to Bourbon Street later to hit a few spots now that the tourists aren't taking over," Pansy volunteered. "You could come if you want."

Sully knew exactly how to respond. "I'll ask my fiancée when I see her later. If she's up for it, we'll totally see you there."

Pansy's disappointment was obvious. "Oh, well, okay."

"Talk to you later." Sully headed straight for the lab. He knocked before entering and waited for Ted Caldwell to invite him in.

"Is this your case?" Ted asked when Sully joined him.

"It is." Sully couldn't stop himself from fixating on

Cobra, who was open on the table. He'd seen a lot of death in his time, but it was still jarring on occasion. "Anything?"

"Well, your victims weren't in the best of health."

"Living on the street does that to you," Sully replied dryly. "That's not exactly earth-shattering news."

"No." Caldwell rolled his neck. "I can tell you the one they call Godzilla would've been dead within the year. He had stomach cancer, and obviously wasn't getting any treatment for it. He would've gone downhill fast anyway. He was probably already feeling as if things were about as terrible as they could possibly get."

"They can always get worse," Sully mused.

"They can," Caldwell agreed. "He was about to be in a lot of pain, though. I'm not sure this wasn't better for him. My guess is he was already in pain and had nothing but alcohol to combat it."

Sully felt inexplicably sad thinking about it. "Well, that is not what I wanted to hear, but I guess that's one silver lining. Anything else?"

"I can tell you that the other two both had livers that were seriously overtaxed."

"Again, that's not exactly earth-shattering news."

"None of them died from the knife wounds," Caldwell volunteered. "Does that interest you?"

Sully nodded without hesitation. "Now that interests me. I figured they didn't die from being stabbed. There was no blood on the scene, and a witness said she saw them walking not long before they would've died. Or, when I'm guessing they would've died."

"Time of death for all three is around ten o'clock last night," Caldwell volunteered. "As for what they died of, well, I'm not sure."

Sully rested his hands on his hips. "How can you not be sure? They were clearly murdered, right?"

"Um ... I don't know." Caldwell shifted from one foot to the other. His discomfort was obvious. "The thing is, I think it's possible they all died of heart attacks maybe. There are markers suggesting heart attacks."

"But?"

"But what are the odds they all died of heart attacks?"

"Not good. I guarantee they didn't all die of heart attacks, somehow stab themselves after the fact, and arrange their bodies in a pinwheel."

"I would agree with that." Caldwell made an attempt at a smile. It didn't touch his eyes. "I've sent samples in for toxicology results. I'm going to have another coroner come in and take a look. Right now, though, I don't have anything definitive to put down on my report."

Sully studied Caldwell for several seconds. It was obvious the coroner was keeping something from him. "What aren't you telling me?" he asked finally.

"I'm telling you that if I was forced to give an answer as to what killed them at this point, you wouldn't like what I had to say."

"And that would be?"

"Fright," Caldwell replied. "I think they died of fright. They were obviously very frightened at the end. They might not have known what was going to happen with the knives and the posing, but they were afraid ... and I think they might have been afraid enough that it killed them."

Sully had no idea what to make of that. "Well ... okay," he said finally. He touched his tongue to his top lip. "How soon are you going to bring in the other coroner?"

Caldwell let loose a harsh laugh. "Is that your way of telling me that you don't believe my take on the subject?"

"That's my way of saying I would love to hear a second opinion."

"I don't blame you." Caldwell was rueful. "I've never seen anything like this."

"You're not the only one."

# 8

## EIGHT

Ofelia checked in at the front desk of her father's hospital. The receptionist recognized her on sight now and waved her back. Dr. Clark Welling was waiting outside Oscar's room for her when she made her way down the hallway, and the sinking feeling that threatened to overtake Ofelia had her slowing her pace.

"He's taken a step back," she assumed as she arrived at the doctor's side.

"No." Welling shook his head. "In fact, he's having a great day. I was considering calling you to stop by, so you could see for yourself, but since I'm hopeful that he continues to have great days, I didn't want to make a big deal out of it."

Ofelia let loose the breath she hadn't even realized she was holding. "I know it's stupid to get worked up about this stuff because he's still going to have bad days, but I'm grateful things are going well right now, and I don't want to break the streak."

"I understand." Welling shot her a sympathetic smile. "Your father is a work in progress. Not everything is going to be easy for him going forward—and he will have bad days—but it should be better than what it was before. That's what we're going for here."

"I get it." Ofelia didn't have to force a smile, which was a distinct change from how things had been when Oscar was first transferred to the hospital. "Can I see him? I don't have a lot of time—I have to get to Krewe—but I would like to spend twenty minutes or so with him."

"Knock yourself out. I'm sure he'll be glad to see you."

Ofelia said her goodbyes to Welling and knocked on her father's open door before entering. She wanted to respect his privacy as much as possible and was gratified when he immediately jumped up from the table he'd been sitting at and raced toward her.

"I didn't know you were coming today." He pulled her in for a bear hug, which was the most effusive greeting he'd managed in weeks, and he was all smiles when he pulled back.

Ofelia was another story, however. Tears brimmed in her eyes, and they were in danger of falling.

"Oh, what's wrong with you?" Oscar looked horrified. "Did that jerk you insist on living with do something to you? I'll thump him good." He brandished his fist as proof.

Ofelia laughed and swiped at the tears. It was stupid to cry. She was just so happy about Oscar's current mood. No, it wouldn't last. It couldn't. She wouldn't love him any less on his bad days. She was going to take this win, though.

"There's nothing wrong with Zach," she assured him. "Things with us are great."

Oscar looked disappointed. "I guess that's good." His tone told her he felt otherwise. "How is your brother's new bar?"

"It's going really well." Ofelia sat in the chair next to

him. "Felix is excited about the drinks he's creating. He's even paying extra to Zach every month. Business is good."

"Except we're going into the down period," Oscar noted. He'd run Krewe for years before Ofelia purchased it from him. He was well aware of the ebbs and flows of the bar business in New Orleans.

"He has it under control," Ofelia assured him. "We outsourced half his staff through a temp agency when he first opened because we knew he wouldn't be able to keep all of his workers throughout the winter months. Once Halloween passes, he'll drop the temp agency, and he'll have half his regular staff for several months. Then, before Mardi Gras, he'll bulk up again."

"Then natural attrition should set in," Oscar surmised. "That's good. That's really, really good."

"It is," Ofelia agreed. "As soon as you're out, the first place I'll take you is Archer. I promise. You're going to love it."

Oscar nodded, his hand moving to his jaw so he could rub it. He didn't shave every day—more like every other day —so there was salt and pepper stubble present today.

"Is something wrong?" Ofelia queried, reading the change in his body language.

"I don't know if you would say anything is wrong," Oscar hedged. "It's just ... um ... about getting out of here."

Ofelia's stomach sank. "I don't think it's time just yet." Oscar had stopped begging to go home a few weeks before. That didn't mean he was ready to go home anytime soon. He needed more time at the hospital. She was sure of it.

"It's not that." Oscar fervently shook his head. "It's just ... you know that counseling is part of the program here, right?"

Ofelia wasn't certain where he was going with this, but

she nodded all the same. "I am aware of that. You haven't wanted to talk about the counseling so far, though."

"That's because it's stupid. I don't like talking about my feelings constantly. They say it's good for me, though."

"Have you been talking about your feelings?" Ofelia queried.

"Some, I guess. I thought I was getting by. However, they have made it clear that they believe I need a few family sessions, so they can understand the dynamic I'm living with on the outside."

"Oh." Realization dawned on Ofelia. "I didn't know that was a thing."

"It's a stupid thing."

"Maybe, but if they think you need it…"

"They said they want to be able to identify triggers so they can have a plan in place to deal with them when it's time to leave," he said. "I already know what my triggers are. I don't need them helping me to point out other things. They think it's best, though."

"Do you know when they want to do this?"

"Not yet. They said they were going to call you. I just wanted to make you aware that they're going to call you."

"Okay, well, I'll deal with it." Ofelia flashed a smile that she didn't feel. "Are they going to shrink Felix and me too?" She was freaked out at the prospect.

"I have no idea, but if they crawl into your head, it's hard to get them out."

"Well … we'll figure it out." No matter what, Ofelia would do whatever was necessary to make sure her father was going to be prepared for what was to come. "Now, tell me what else is going on. Also, if you've seen any mimes, I need to know about it."

. . .

**OSCAR, THANKFULLY, HADN'T SEEN ANY** mimes. He promised Ofelia he would have the hospital staff contact her right away if that changed. When she left, she was feeling lighter than she had since the incident with Sully the previous evening. Her euphoria only lasted until she walked through the door of Krewe and found her mother holding court at a table with several women she didn't recognize. They were all wearing white tracksuits.

"Oh, son of a witch," Ofelia lamented as she threw her purse on the bar counter and glared in her mother's direction.

"It doesn't sound as if you're happy to see me," a male voice said from Ofelia's right, drawing her gaze in that direction. When she realized exactly who was sitting at her bar—how had she missed him upon initial entry?—she let loose a heavy sigh. "And here I thought things were going so well," she lamented.

Zeke let loose a hearty laugh as he tipped back his drink and finished it off. He slammed the glass on the bar with a flourish. "Barkeep, I'll have another."

Jaxson Mulgrew, a local kid Ofelia had always been fond of, was working behind the bar. He tilted his head, his turquoise hair catching the light, and snagged gazes with Ofelia. "Am I the barkeep in this scenario?"

"Ignore him," Ofelia replied. Her agitation was obvious. "I've got this." She stomped around to the other side of the bar so she could enter the interior, where she proceeded to grab an apron before moving to stand in front of Zeke. When she found him looking inside her purse, her temper got the best of her.

"Manners!" she snapped as she grabbed his wrist, zinging enough magic through him to cause him to go rigid on his stool. That allowed her to grab her purse and shove it in the cubby beneath the bar.

As for Zeke, his hair was standing on end when she caught his gaze again. "What will it be?" she asked in innocent fashion.

"Holy Zamboni," Zeke snapped when he could get his tongue working again. "What did you just do to me?"

"Very little," Ofelia replied. "If you keep acting like a tool, you'll find out how much worse it can get."

"That sounds ominous."

"Oh, it is." Ofelia wasn't in the mood to deal with Zeke. She had no doubt he was operating with ulterior motives. Her problem was that she wasn't in the mood to deal with her mother either. It was like *Sophie's Choice* ... but with no sign of a good outcome either way. "What do you want?"

"That is no way to speak to your future father-in-law, young lady."

"What do you want?" Ofelia repeated.

Zeke let loose a long-suffering sigh. "I'll have a Mint Julep."

Ofelia froze, multiple questions fighting for supremacy in her mind. "First up, I was asking a general 'what are you doing here in my bar' question because I don't believe you really stopped by for a drink," she said. "Secondly ... really? A Mint Julep? My grandmother called and referred to you as an old lady for your drink choice."

Zeke's lips curved up. "I can see what my son sees in you. You're fiery."

"Oh, geez." Ofelia grabbed a cup so she could muddle mint, powdered sugar, and water in it. She barely moved her gaze from Zeke. "Are you here to cause trouble for Zach? I swear, you're not going to like it if you upset him. We have enough going on without adding whatever you have planned to the mix."

"What makes you think I have something planned?"

"Let's just say I'm used to parents who like to plot."

"Ah, your mentally ill father." Zeke bobbed his head. "I've heard about him."

Ofelia's eyes narrowed to slits. "Don't refer to my father that way." Her voice was low and deadly. "Don't ever refer to him that way again."

Zeke looked taken aback. "I didn't mean anything by it." He raised his hands in supplication. "I was just joking. That's what we do in my family."

"About mental illness?" Ofelia grabbed a bottle of bourbon.

"My grandfather liked to wear chaps with nothing underneath them," Zeke explained. "He would go out into the yard with his gun and shoot gators. All the while he would insist you had to call him Wyatt Earp. It wasn't a huge problem until he tried tying red bandanas to the gators and started losing limbs."

Ofelia added bourbon to the cup before returning the bottle to the rack and grabbing another mint sprig to use as a garnish. "Is that story true?" she asked finally.

"Yes. We have a bunch of whackadoodles in our family. We deal with it by expressing ourselves with humor."

"And you think that helps?"

"It's better than tears."

Ofelia considered it a beat and then nodded as she handed over the cocktail. "This is still a gross drink. I appreciate your take on the situation though."

Zeke sipped and shot her a thumbs-up. "Perfection." He lowered the glass, and for the first time since she'd met him, Ofelia realized he wasn't showing any outward signs of putting on an act. "I'm sorry about your father," he offered. "I don't know all the specifics. My wife said you love him, and you feel guilt for putting him in a home."

"A hospital," Ofelia corrected. "He's in a hospital getting treatment. His home is elsewhere, and he'll be going back to it."

Zeke studied her for several seconds, perhaps taking in the stubborn tilt of her head, and then nodded. "I'm sure things will go your way."

"They will." Ofelia darted a look toward her mother and frowned when she saw the women whispering to one another, heads bent together. It was obvious they were up to no good.

"Maybe they're in a cult," Zeke suggested as he followed her gaze. "I mean ... how else would you explain their outfits?"

"They're part of a walking group. They call themselves the White Walkers."

Abject horror washed over Zeke's features. "You can't be serious." He was aghast.

His reaction was enough to earn a real grin from Ofelia. "I'm afraid so."

"Have they seen *Game of Thrones?*"

Ofelia shook her head. "I can guarantee none of those women have ever watched a show that involves removing penises and hooking up with your twin brother."

Zeke chuckled. "That was a very good show. Well, up until the end. There were a few issues with the end."

"Yes. They didn't name themselves after the show, though."

"And what did they name themselves for?"

"Well, they're white ... and they're walking ... and they like to report any crime they find."

This time the horror that cascaded across Zeke's face was of a different variety. "You cannot be serious."

"Oh, but I am."

"They told you this?" He took another drink of his Mint Julep.

Ofelia cast another look toward her mother. "I had inside information, so to speak."

"That sounds like a story."

"Not a good one." Ofelia braced herself when her mother got up from the table and started in her direction. "I just knew it," she hissed under her breath. Despite her annoyance, she fixed her mother with a bright smile. "Do you need a fresh cocktail?" she asked in a voice that was much shriller than her normal voice.

Zeke gave her an odd look but didn't say anything.

"I would like a white wine spritzer," Marie replied.

"Ah, so even your drinks are white now," Ofelia drawled. She rummaged in the refrigerator until she came back with some white wine and poured it in a glass. "I don't like to pick," she started, then internally cringed when she realized she sounded like her mother. "Wait. That came out wrong."

Clearly fascinated, Zeke sipped his Mint Julep and watched the show.

"If you have something to say, Ofelia, just say it."

"Fine." Ofelia spritzed some soda in her mother's white wine. "I don't like your friends, and I don't want them here." Ofelia plastered a huge smile on her face as she handed the spritz to her mother. "Cheers."

Marie rolled her eyes. "They haven't done anything to

you. They're actually doing a lot of good for the community."

"Name one good thing they've done," Ofelia challenged.

"They're cleaning up the neighborhoods. They're getting ahead of the crime."

"You mean they're calling the cops whenever they see someone black," Ofelia countered.

"That is a gross lie!" Marie's eyes filled with fire. "You take that back."

"I'm good," Ofelia replied. She was in no mood for her mother's shenanigans. "Why don't you guys head over to Felix's new bar and bug him. I'm sure he would love to mix white wine and soda for you."

If looks could kill, Ofelia would be dead. Marie's annoyance with her offspring was so palpable it could've been bottled and sold as musk. "I'll have you know that we visited your brother yesterday. As your mother, I feel it's my job to visit you today. I like to spread the love around."

"Oh, is that what you're doing?" Ofelia wanted to crawl into bed and take a nap. "I guess I'll have to take your word for it."

"This is your mother?" Zeke interjected. He looked delighted.

Ofelia shot him a quelling look. "Don't make things weird. I barely know you, but I'm guessing you're good at making things weird."

"Very good," Zeke agreed. He turned his full attention to Marie. "I'm Topher Sully. You can call me Zeke, though."

"Topher Sully?" Marie's eyes sparkled. "The Topher Sully who owns the new drilling rig off the coast? The one that employs three hundred people in high-paying positions?"

"Oh, geez." Ofelia was at the end of her rope. "Since when do you care about people getting jobs?"

Marie ignored her. "You have quite the reputation. I'm so glad to meet you. What..." Before she could ask the obvious question, Marie trailed off. "Wait ... Sully." She turned her attention to Ofelia. "Is this Zach's father?"

It was the sort of question Ofelia didn't want to answer. She had no choice, though. "Yes, and don't get weird about it."

"I'm just shocked. I had no idea that Zacharias came from such an acclaimed family." Marie turned a flirty smile toward Zeke. "Your son obviously inherited his charming personality from you."

"Someone pass me a barf bag," Ofelia drawled. Her mother was well aware that Sully was from a rich family. She'd mentioned it incessantly after meeting his mother. Now she was just playing a game.

"Nobody needs your negativity," Marie snapped. There was a warning in her gaze when it snagged with Ofelia's annoyed stare. When she turned back to Zeke, the charm Ofelia often forgot she possessed was on full display. "How long are you in town?"

"Oh, I'm working on a business deal," Zeke replied. "I'm not quite certain. I'm hopeful that things will come together sooner rather than later. It's not going well, though."

"Well, I insist we have a family dinner tonight," Marie said.

Ofelia had been anticipating it. That didn't make her any less annoyed when the words escaped Marie's mouth. "I'm busy."

"Doing what?"

"Spending quality time with my fiancé."

"And this is your fiancé's father." Marie gestured toward Zeke. "I think a family dinner is in order since he's only in town for a limited time. I mean ... what sort of message do you want to send, Ofelia? We're good hostesses, no matter what you think or say. I refuse to let your poor example ruin my stellar reputation."

Ofelia's lower lip came out to play, and Zeke didn't bother to hide his smile as he regarded her.

"I think a family dinner sounds lovely," Zeke said out of the blue.

Ofelia murdered him with a death glare. "Oh, I'm going to make you cry before this trip is over with," she growled.

"Lovely." Marie beamed at him. "I'll pick a restaurant and make a reservation. I'm doubtful Felix will be able to get away, so it will just be the five of us. I'll text Ofelia with the details."

"I'm looking forward to it," Zeke assured her. His smile never diminished as he watched Marie flounce back to her table. "Your mother seems interesting."

"Yeah, you're not going to be saying that when she's ruthlessly questioning you over dinner at some fancy schmancy place with linen napkins."

"I happen to like fancy schmancy food."

"Of course you do." Ofelia briefly closed her eyes. "Who would've thought my father would ever be the only one not causing me stress?" she asked finally.

"I have no idea," Zeke replied. "Do you want to talk about your stress?"

"Not really."

"Good. Then you can tell me all about your relationship with my son. I feel as if I've been left in the dark regarding some of the details."

"That doesn't sound much better as a conversational topic."

"You'll live. Let's start with how you met and go from there."

"It's going to be a long afternoon, isn't it?"

"Yes, but it will be worth it."

"For you or me?"

"Does it matter?"

# 9
## NINE

Ofelia dressed in a simple black dress with spaghetti straps and a moderate heel. She would've foregone the heel and gone with flats if she wasn't having dinner with her mother. She knew darned well her mother would cause a scene if she wore anything with less than a two-inch heel.

"You look nice." Sully looked over from his spot next to the dresser, where he was straightening his tie, and took in his fiancée with an appreciative eye. "Have I mentioned that you're my favorite person in the world today?"

"I don't know." Ofelia's reaction was dull. "Maybe."

Sully dropped his hands and regarded her. "Are you going to be surly all night? If so, I can call and cancel. I can tell them you're sick."

Ofelia was feeling sick. Not sick enough to get out of dinner with her mother, though. "It's fine." She turned back to the bathroom, intent on running the brush through her hair again. Then she paused. "Am I the only one who thinks having a dinner with my mother and your father is a terrible idea?"

Sully shrugged. "They're going to meet each other eventually, Ofelia. We're getting married. They'll both be at the wedding."

"Not if we elope."

Sully chuckled. "I'm all for eloping. We can elope right now if you want. The problem is, that's not what you want."

"You don't know." Ofelia's forehead creased. "I could want that."

"No, you want your father to walk you down the aisle. You want a crawfish cake. You want gumbo as an appetizer and a good old-fashioned crawfish boil as the main course." He was smiling when he turned back to her. "You don't want anything fancy, but you do want it to feel like our city threw a party just for us."

Ofelia swallowed hard. He knew her so well. It was daunting sometimes. "If I tell you something, do you promise not to get mad?" It wasn't the best transition she'd ever managed, but she was feeling guilty.

"No. I promise to love you no matter what, though. That should be enough."

On a sigh, Ofelia nodded. "I don't like your father."

Sully waited for her to continue. When she didn't, he grinned. "That's it? That's your big secret?"

"He's your father. I'm supposed to like him."

"There's no rule that says that." He crossed to her. "It's not as if I like your mother."

"You're polite to her. I can't always be polite to your father for some reason. It's as if he pushes every negative button I have."

"I'm not always nice to your mother either." Sully kissed the tip of her nose. "You don't have to feel any specific way about my father," he said as he pulled back. "You're marrying me. Not him."

Ofelia didn't really see it that way, but she nodded all the same. "Okay. You know this dinner is going to be hellish, right?"

"I *do* know that." Sully bobbed his head. "I figure things will be so tense nobody will stay for dessert, so it will be over in an hour. Then we'll take dessert home and eat it in bed and wash away the tension with a little ... playtime." His smile was impish.

"That's what you think, huh?"

"That's what I think."

Despite her insistence on remaining tense, Ofelia grinned. "Okay, then. Let's have a dinner with my mother and your father." She slipped her hand into his. "Be prepared to pretend I'm sick if they're unbearable before the entrees."

"I'll have a puke story at the ready."

"At least you have a plan."

"Like the best Boy Scout, I'm always prepared," he agreed.

**MARIE CHOSE THE ORIGINAL PIERRE MASPERO'S** for their dinner. Ofelia had always been a fan of the food, even if she thought the name was overblown.

Marie and her husband Henri were already at a table when Ofelia and Sully entered the establishment on Chartres Street, so there was no containing Ofelia's sigh as the hostess led them toward the table.

"Hello." Marie beamed at Sully and held out her cheek for him to kiss, which he did.

Ofelia leaned over the table and hugged Henri. Even though Ofelia found spending time with her mother trying, her stepfather was a different story. He'd never been anything but lovely. "How are you?" she asked him.

"Good." Henri beamed at her. "Business is slow right now, but I'm okay with that. We'll have the big push for Halloween week and then the slow slide through the holidays. I know I need to make money—and I appreciate high season—but I like the quiet time as well."

"I do, too," Ofelia agreed. "It's like the next three months allow me to breathe and catch up."

"Are you guys planning on going anywhere during the break?" Marie queried. Her eyes had moved to the front of the restaurant, to where Zeke was making his presence known, but she turned her attention back to her daughter fairly quickly.

"I hadn't really thought about it," Ofelia admitted. "Probably not."

"Hold up." Sully straightened in his chair. "I thought we agreed we wanted to get some travel in when we could arrange it."

"We did," Ofelia replied. "I just don't think it's happening this season."

"And why is that?" Sully flicked his eyes to his father as the man approached. He didn't greet him, however. Instead, he kept his focus on Ofelia.

"Because..." She didn't immediately expand.

"Because what?" Sully prodded.

"Good evening," Zeke greeted everyone. "What a lovely place. I'm assuming you chose it," he said to Marie on a dimpled smile.

"I did," Marie confirmed. "I'm glad you approve." She

held out her hand for him to kiss, which only served to turn Ofelia's stomach.

Sully was still fixated on his fiancée. "Why can't we go somewhere for a vacation, Fe? I was making plans for the first week of January. I wanted to surprise you."

Ofelia was taken aback. "Oh, well ... um ... I would love to go on vacation with you."

"Then why aren't we going on vacation?" Sully refused to let it go.

"We'll talk about it later," Ofelia replied, refusing to make eye contact.

"No, I want to talk about it now. You'll try to distract me with nudity later, and I want an answer."

"You should take the nudity," Zeke said sagely. "Trust me. You might think you get plenty of the nudity now, so the vacation is more important, but you'll want the nudity in a year when she closes up shop and turns to nagging."

Sully pinned his father with a death glare. "Is that what my mother did to you?"

"Oh, I'm not answering that," Zeke replied as he grabbed the menu to take a look. "You're something of a mama's boy and will tell her if I say anything of the sort."

Sully muttered something unintelligible under his breath.

"I'm going to have the Bohemian Julep," Zeke decided. "It sounds fun."

Ofelia shot him a dirty look. "What is it with you and mint?"

"It's a lovely choice," Marie assured him. "I'm getting that too."

"I'm getting the Marie Laveau in a vat," Ofelia replied.

"You're going to tell me why we can't go on the vacation

I've been planning first," Sully replied. "I want to be able to travel, Ofelia. I thought you wanted that too."

"I do." Ofelia hated—*absolutely hated*—that they were having this conversation in front of an audience. She knew Sully wasn't just going to let it go, though. "It's just ... I want to wait to make plans to see when my dad might be getting out. They said he might be out in time for Christmas, although they refuse to give me any firm dates."

Realization washed over Sully, and he unclenched. She wasn't backing out on their plans. She was just trying to make sure that Oscar's reintroduction to society went as smoothly as possible. "Oh." He ran his tongue over his lips. "I didn't think about that." He flicked his eyes to the approaching server as he debated how to respond. "I'll have the Grey Goose Martini," he said.

"The Loosey Goosey Martini?" the server queried.

A muscle worked in Sully's jaw. "Yes, but I refuse to call it that." He waited for the others to place their drink orders to speak again. "I didn't think about your father's release from the hospital. We don't have to travel this year." He took her hand. "I'm going to want to travel next year, though." His gaze was searching as it roamed her face.

"I want to travel too," she assured him. "I just ... I'm nervous about my father's release."

"Have you seen him recently?" Marie asked. She made a point of pretending she was disinterested in hearing the answer, but Ofelia could tell that was far from true.

"I saw him today," Ofelia replied. "He's doing really well."

"I didn't realize you were visiting him today," Marie replied. "I thought tomorrow was your normal day."

"And I didn't realize you were watching my visitation days so closely," Ofelia fired back. "Tomorrow is my normal day, but given what happened with the mimes ... well ... I wanted to make sure he was okay."

"And he was?" Sully pressed.

"He was," Ofelia confirmed. She flipped the menu to the food options. "He wants to have a family counseling session. Actually, the doctors do. It's part of the process, so we're aware of what could trigger him when he's released."

"Well, just tell me when they want to do it, and I'll make sure that I save a spot in my schedule," Sully said. "We'll work it out."

Ofelia let loose a breath. "Really?" She couldn't help being dubious. "I promised you a trip in the next few months, *and* now I'm disappointing you and asking you to go to family counseling for my father, and you're still being pleasant? What's that about?"

"You did, but you can't control everything. I think it's important to get your dad squared away. We can't expect Felix to watch him and take care of a new bar at the same time. I can move my trip planning until next year."

That seemed far too easy to Ofelia. She smiled all the same. "Thank you."

"Don't mention it." Sully pressed a kiss to her temple and then focused on the menu. "They have fried green tomatoes," he said after a beat. "Your favorite."

Ofelia nodded. "One of them at least. I think I'm going to order those."

Sully moved his hand to her back so he could lightly rub away the stress she was feeling. "We can split them as an appetizer if you want."

"That sounds good."

The table dissolved into silence. After several seconds, Ofelia looked up. "What?" she demanded, irritation with their dinner guests on full display.

"Nothing." Marie shook her head. "You guys are just so in tune with one another. It's kind of sweet."

"Yes, it reminds me of one of those high school television shows," Zeke agreed. "Who doesn't love Joanie and Chachi?"

Sully glared at his father. "Figure out what you want for dinner and stop being condescending," he ordered.

Zeke was the picture of innocence when he raised his chin. "What did I say?"

Marie waved off his question. "Ignore them. They're sensitive."

"Apparently so. Your daughter is still upset because she saw my penis last night. I mean ... get over it. Am I right?" He sent Marie a saucy smile.

Rather than agree, Marie frowned. "What now?"

"Oh, geez." Ofelia sank down in her chair. She forced herself to stare at her menu. "I'm thinking I might get the Crawfish Étouffée. Either that or the Seafood Pot Pie." She was desperate when she turned to Sully. To her horror, he was grinning. "It's not funny," she insisted.

Sully chuckled. "Maybe not to you, but I find the whole thing entertaining."

"How did she see your penis?" Marie queried.

"I cannot have this conversation," Ofelia growled. She tapped Sully's menu. "You should get the Seafood Pot Pie."

"So you can eat half of it?" Sully queried. "If you want it, you should get it because I want the Blackened Redfish."

Ofelia made a face. "What is it with you and fish? You actually like it."

"It was a regular delicacy in our house growing up. Sorry."

Ofelia involuntarily shuddered.

"You can get the Crawfish Étouffée whenever you

want," he noted. "Almost every place carries it. The Seafood Pot Pie isn't something you can get just anywhere."

Ofelia nodded. He had a point.

"I want to go back to Zeke's penis," Marie prodded.

"Don't we all?" Zeke drawled.

"No," Ofelia and Sully replied at the same time.

"How is it exactly that you saw it?" Marie queried. "I mean ... it's not normal for a woman to just stumble across her future father-in-law's penis, Ofelia. I know that didn't happen to me. Either time."

"Kill me now," Ofelia muttered.

Sully was caught between laughing and consoling her. He didn't know which would go over better. "Um..."

"It was an accident," Zeke volunteered. "It's not a big deal."

"She accidentally saw your penis?" Marie didn't look convinced. "Where did this happen?" She didn't wait for an answer. Instead, she turned toward Ofelia. "If you're having an affair with your future father-in-law, that's entirely inappropriate."

"It wouldn't be much of an affair if I talked about it right in front of Sully, would it?" Ofelia shot back.

"I ... well ... I'm confused." Marie folded her arms across her chest. "I think I need some enlightenment."

"So, so much enlightenment," Ofelia drawled.

"I'm being serious, Ofelia. This is not a good situation."

Sully cleared his throat to draw Marie's attention. "It happened last night. There was an incident when I was working a case. I was injured. My father showed up at the penthouse when Ofelia was taking care of me. There was a misunderstanding with the bathroom."

Marie still looked dubious. "Was it your misunderstanding, young lady, or his?" Marie demanded of her daughter.

"Mine," Zeke replied, lying smoothly. "I didn't realize that the door wasn't latched properly. It's over now, and we're moving past it."

"Except it somehow keeps popping up in conversation," Sully muttered.

Ofelia pressed her lips together in an effort to keep from laughing.

"What's so funny?" Sully demanded.

"Nothing," she assured him quickly. "It's just ... you said it kept popping up."

"I didn't realize you were a twelve-year-old boy disguised as a beautiful woman," Sully muttered. Despite himself, now he was fighting a grin. "Unbelievable." He shook his head. "I can't believe you're making me act like a twelve-year-old boy now."

"I'm getting the Blackened Gulf Shrimp Alfredo Pasta," Henri volunteered out of nowhere.

"Oh, you shouldn't eat heavy cream like that," Marie chided. "You'll give yourself a heart attack."

"That's what I'm getting," Zeke countered. "If I die of a heart attack, what a way to go, right?" He gave Henri a wink. "The only thing that would make it better is a stripper sitting on my lap while I eat it."

All traces of mirth had fled Marie's features, and she openly glared at Zeke. "Do you think that's funny?" she demanded.

He shrugged. "Maybe a little funny. What? Are you saying you don't? You need to lighten up, Mary. I'm a funny guy."

"Marie," she corrected icily. "My name is Marie."

Zeke's face was blank. "What did I say?"

Ofelia angled her body toward Sully. "Well, I don't think we have to worry about them being best buds," she said in a low voice.

"Were you legitimately worried about that?" Sully queried.

She shrugged. "Maybe a little. My mother can be charming when she wants to be, and she saw dollar signs the second she registered who your father was."

Sully captured her chin and gave her a kiss. "Do you know what I see when I look at you?"

"Hearts?" Ofelia teased.

"How did you know?"

"Because I see them when I look at you too."

They exchanged a sweet kiss. After a few seconds, over which they allowed it to linger, they both looked up to find the others at the table watching them.

"What?" Ofelia asked blankly.

"That's not appropriate restaurant behavior, Ofelia," Marie chided, although her tone lacked its usual bite. "Also, we should really start planning for your wedding. Any ideas when you want it to be?"

Ofelia had given that some thought. "Not until Dad is out of the hospital."

"What if your father never gets out of the hospital?" Marie held up her hand to still Ofelia before her daughter got a full head of steam and exploded. "I'm not saying that's what I want to happen. I'm just saying it's possible."

"It's not possible," Ofelia countered. "He's getting out. I saw him today. He was great. I know he'll have issues when he leaves, but I also believe that we're going to make it work. I want him at my wedding."

"He's going to be there," Sully assured her. He sent Marie a warning look. "We haven't talked about the specifics of the wedding much. I was thinking maybe we could have it in Jackson Square, though. That's one of our favorite spots."

"They won't let you do weddings in Jackson Square during tourist season," Marie argued.

"Not during the day," Sully agreed. "I was thinking we might have it at night, though. A lot of our friends are night people."

Ofelia broke out into a grin. "I like that idea."

"I thought you might." He stroked his hand over her hair. "We don't have to make a decision right now. We'll get through the family counseling and then start hashing things out. If we don't get married for a few months, it's fine. We'll just keep living in sin."

"Ugh." Marie made a disgusted sound in her throat. "You just had to phrase it that way, didn't you?"

"I really did," Sully agreed on a laugh. He loved agitating his future mother-in-law. "There's no hurry. We're happy. Once we know more about Oscar's timetable, we'll start talking about wedding details."

"I don't suppose anybody wants my take on the subject," Zeke prodded.

"No," Sully replied, not missing a beat. "We really don't want your take on the subject. Order your food and stop making things uncomfortable."

"Fine." Zeke didn't look happy, but he nodded all the same. "This is a very strange dinner, though. I've never sat through anything remotely like it."

"You'll live," Sully fired back. "That's how it is with family. Things are always uncomfortable ... until they're not."

"I guess, but your mother wouldn't like this."

"My mother isn't here," Sully reminded him. "She's sat through a dinner like this anyway. She understands."

"Well, she didn't warn me."

"No, she didn't." Sully turned thoughtful. He couldn't help but wonder why his mother hadn't prepared his father for something like this. That was very unlike her. Something else was going on. He could feel it.

# 10

## TEN

Ofelia and Sully didn't order dessert despite their earlier plans. Instead, the second dinner was over with, they excused themselves to walk through the French Quarter. They needed the emotional break. And, truth be told, they were on the lookout for mimes.

Neither of them came right out and said they wanted to hit the riverwalk because they were desperate to find the enemy. Instead, they ambled in that direction. Nobody said anything, not even when they were climbing the steps after Ofelia had magically switched out her shoes to something more comfortable, and once the breeze hit them at the top of the stairs, they both sucked in a much-needed breath.

"What are you thinking?" Sully asked as Ofelia looked left and right, up and down the riverwalk.

"I'm thinking that, for once, my mother was not the most annoying parent at the table," Ofelia replied. She cast Sully a sidelong look. "What's up with your dad?"

Rather than immediately answer, Sully went to the railing to look out on the dark water of the Mississippi. He was tired—oh, so very tired—but he knew this was a conversation that needed to be held. "He's not as bad as you think," he started.

"I should hope so. If he was as bad as I've been thinking, I would have to kill him."

Sully arched an eyebrow. "That's some bold talk."

"Maybe, but he's terrible. Like ... horrible. It's not in a funny way either. Sometimes my mom is so bad, she's funny. Your mother is the same way. Your father, though..."

"He's an acquired taste," Sully agreed.

"It didn't occur to me that you almost never talked about your father until he was in our apartment last night," she admitted. "Now I understand why."

"I don't hate my father," Sully assured her.

"Of course you don't. He's your father. You love him despite his faults."

"I'm just not close to him," Sully insisted. "I mean ... you've met him. He's a hard man to bond with. My mother is difficult more often than not, but I'm still bonded with her. She feels like a real person. My father doesn't feel like a real person sometimes."

Ofelia was interested despite herself. "What does he feel like?"

"He's like the father on a television show from back in the day. He's there, but he's not often present. He's always at work because the job of raising the children is women's work."

"You're saying he's sexist," Ofelia deduced.

"Yes, but if you were to ask him if he was sexist, he would say he wasn't ... and he would probably pass a polygraph on the subject," Sully replied. "He doesn't have malice for women. Everything he feels is simply part of his

DNA. Like ... he doesn't understand why a woman wouldn't be happy sitting at home and raising children."

"I kind of want to punch him," Ofelia lamented.

Sully chuckled. "You would not be the first person to say that. My mother often wants to punch him."

"But they're still married," Ofelia pressed. "They've been together for thirty-five years or whatever, and they're still together."

"Yes, but my father travels seventy-five percent of the time," Sully pointed out. "He comes home maybe one or two days a week. I'm pretty sure he has his own bedroom at this point."

"They sleep in separate rooms?" Ofelia found she was intrigued. "Does your dad...?" She didn't finish it out. Mostly because she believed there was no way to do it delicately.

"I have no idea," Sully replied, reading her perfectly. "On the face of it, I would assume he does cheat on my mother. The thing is, I can also see him playing the martyr. He might flirt with whichever woman in a small skirt flits in front of him, but that doesn't necessarily mean he's taking her back to his hotel room."

"Was he a good father to you?" Ofelia asked.

"Not like your father. He never abused me or anything, though."

"That's not necessarily being a good father," Ofelia noted.

"I know. He tried, to the extent of his limited ability. That's the best I can say for him. My mother did most of the rearing. My father was just the gregarious guy who showed up when we had a play or were winning an award. He was always there for appearance's sake. I think that was some agreement he and my mother struck together."

Ofelia nodded. It made an odd sort of sense. "You said I would like your father," she reminded him. "Back when your mother came to visit, you said I would like your father better."

"Well, I had no way of knowing that your first vision of my father would include full-frontal nudity." Sully cracked a smile, but it didn't last. "I know, Fe, there's something off about him this trip. He's even more off than usual. I can't put my finger on it."

Ofelia had wondered, but she hadn't wanted to push. Not when they had other things on their mind. "Maybe it's because you sense things might have changed between your parents and you instinctively want to protect her," she suggested.

"Why would you assume that?"

"Because it's obvious she hasn't been sharing information with him about us. That's kind of a red flag to me."

Sully touched his tongue to his top lip, debating, then nodded. "I noticed that too. He's in the dark. It's not a good thing, whatever it is. I don't know what to make of it."

"I'm going to tell you something you told me when I was struggling with my father," she said in a soft voice. "We are not responsible for our parents. We're only responsible for ourselves."

"I don't actually disagree with that." He shot her a rueful smile. "I just don't know how I feel about any of it."

"Who says you have to feel anything? Maybe you just have to worry about yourself and leave the rest of it to him to figure out."

Sully studied her for a moment before his expression softened and he extended a hand to her. "I think that's a very good idea. Now, come over here and kiss me."

Ofelia gave him a dubious look. "We're supposed to be hunting mimes, not playing Spin the Bottle."

"Oh, you're the only one I want to kiss," he assured her. "The bottle will only spin toward you."

Ofelia was halfway to handing herself over to him when Sully leaned over and pressed his hand to his stomach. He was obviously feeling discomfort, which was enough to have Ofelia switching gears.

"What's wrong?" she asked as she appeared at his side. "Is it the fish? I bet it's the fish. I told you fish was gross."

"You always think it's the fish," he gritted out. "It's not the fish, though. It's ... something else. I'm not sure how to describe it."

"Do you need me to get you to the hospital?"

"No. It's not that kind of feeling. It's just ... oh, God." Sully's knees almost went out from under him as he grabbed the railing and tried to hold on.

Ofelia kept him up through sheer force of will. "Tell me," she ordered. She was starting to panic. This wasn't some quick bout of food poisoning. No, this was something else.

"It's my father," Sully replied. He looked anguished. "I don't know how I know, but ... he's in trouble. Right now, if I don't get to him, he's going to die."

Ofelia held his gaze for a beat. She didn't have any trouble believing him. She was just confused. "That's what happened to me last night. Where is he?"

"I'm not sure."

Ofelia didn't take a lot of time to think about it. "Stay here," she ordered as she started back toward Jackson Square with a purpose.

"Are you kidding me right now?" Sully yelled at her back.

"Nope. I won't be long. Trust me." With that, she disappeared down the steps, leaving him to twist in the wind as more pain shot through him.

OFELIA COULDN'T KNOW WHERE SHE WOULD find Zeke, and yet she didn't deviate from the direction she'd chosen even once. It was as if she had her own feelings about how things should play out, which is why she wasn't surprised when she found Zeke on the ground at the northeast corner of Jackson Square. He wasn't alone either. He was on his knees, his back pressed to the wrought iron fence posts, and there were three mimes in a half circle in front of him.

It didn't look as if they were having a pleasant conversation.

Ofelia couldn't make out whatever was being said—all the talking was obviously on Zeke's end—but she didn't care what words were being exchanged. She just wanted the pain Sully was in on the other side of the riverwalk steps to dissipate.

"Hey!" she roared as she started across the street, her angle sharp. "Get away from him!" She threw out an arc of magic that had the mimes flying through the air and crashing into the pedestal base where Felix often posed when he was acting as a human statue. The mimes finally made noises, although it was only shrill grunts.

Ofelia jogged across the street—the traffic was stopped at the light—and threw another bit of magic in that direction to keep the light red. The motorists wouldn't like it. She suspected they would start honking and yelling before long. It would give her a bit of time to deal with her current problem without people gawking at her through windows, though.

"Are you okay?" she demanded of Zeke. He had a light sheen of sweat coating his features and looked as if he were about to be sick. That was enough to give Ofelia pause. Had Sully felt his father's injury, or whatever was plaguing him? She didn't think about it too long before she turned her attention back to the mimes. "What will it be, boys?"

The mimes looked caught. Their expressive faces told Ofelia that they hadn't been expecting her appearance ... and perhaps they weren't ready to face off with her after all.

"Make a choice," Ofelia gritted out. "Stay and fight, lose your lives, or go." Part of her wondered if she should let them run. The other part knew she had to secure Zeke's safety, if only because it apparently meant she would be securing Sully's safety as well.

The mimes looked between one another, seemingly debating. Then they backed away from her. They waited until they were a safe distance away to turn back. They bowed in tandem, smiles spreading across their faces. One of them jabbed a finger into the air and twirled it, as if to say, "The world will keep spinning, and we will keep coming." Then they disappeared into the night, heading toward Bourbon Street rather than the riverwalk.

That was a welcome realization to Ofelia.

She turned to Zeke with a purpose and dropped to her knees. Her hands immediately went to the side he was favoring, and when she lifted his shirt, she found blood waiting for her. There was a wound there, but she couldn't tell how deep it was.

"What did they do to you?" she asked in a low voice. "How did they do this I mean? Did they have a knife?"

"Teeth," Zeke replied on a growl. "They used their teeth."

Ofelia's horror knew no bounds. "Are you being serious right now? They bit you?" She couldn't wrap her head around it. "Why would they possibly do that?"

"I can't answer that. You'll have to ask them." Despite his wounded state, Zeke refused to make eye contact. He was fixated on something over Ofelia's shoulder.

When she turned, she found Sully coming down the stairs. He looked winded, his hair standing up all over the place, but he didn't appear to be struggling under the agony of Zeke's wounds any longer. "Over here," she called out.

Sully jerked his head in their direction, seemingly relieved when he saw them. He didn't break into a run, as he normally might have, but he kept up a quick pace. When he reached them, he studied Ofelia first. Finding her none the worse for wear, he focused on his father. "Are you okay?"

"I'll live," Zeke replied on a wan laugh. His breath was ragged. "I need to shift to heal."

Sully nodded. "Yeah."

"Or we could go back to the penthouse," Ofelia argued. "I could give him a potion."

"Baby, shifting will be faster ... and more efficient for a wound that size," Sully replied. "It makes sense for him to shift."

"Oh, man." Ofelia threw her hands into the air. "I'm going to have to see him naked again, aren't I?"

That was enough to elicit a genuine chuckle from Sully. "Actually, that wasn't my plan. I thought maybe you could do a quick walk around the Square, make sure the mimes aren't hanging around, and by the time you get back, he'll be good."

Ofelia's first reaction was to say no. She didn't want to leave them open to attack. Realizing that father and son might need a few minutes together, however, had her nodding. "Okay. Keep your eyes open. I won't be far, but the mimes could still attack."

"I've got it," Sully assured her.

Ofelia glanced between them once more. Then she headed out to make her circle. She tracked her progress by the businesses she passed.

Monty's on the Square. The art gallery. Creole Delicacies. By the time she circled to St. Louis Cathedral, she could breathe easier. She paid special attention to Pirates Alley in case the mimes had decided to flee down there. It was quiet, though.

Then she went back to counting businesses.

Tableau, Chapel Hats, Muse Inspired Fashion, Nola Foot Candy.

Traffic was running normally again when she walked down Decatur. She found Zeke dressed and sitting on a bench, seemingly mostly healed, when she returned.

"No mimes," she announced.

Sully nodded. The concern he'd been harboring when first appearing was seemingly gone. "Did you kill the ones that were here?"

"No, I just scared them off. I needed to focus on your dad."

"Because you were worried about leaving me for too long," he surmised.

"I ... guess." Ofelia couldn't read Sully's emotions very well. That was not normal for her. "Zach, what's wrong?"

Very slowly, very deliberately, Sully turned to her.

"Haven't you figured it out yet? The mimes are hunting my father. That's why they lured me out the way they did last night. They wanted my pain to draw him in. Somehow, they're amplifying our feelings."

Ofelia ran the notion through her head. "But that would mean..." She didn't finish it out. Instead, she moved her eyes to Zeke. "You didn't scent him last night, did you? You weren't out to dinner and just magically scented him, and that's how you stumbled upon us."

Zeke leaned back on the bench. He made a big show of being calm, his arms draped over the back, but Ofelia couldn't ignore the small shudder that ran through him. "I might've been in town a bit longer than I let on," he hedged. "I also might've been drawn to you for reasons other than scent."

Sully exploded. "I knew it! There's no way you just scented me and came running. That's not who you are. If you'd scented me, you would've kept on walking."

"That is not true," Zeke insisted. "I had every intention of visiting you. Eventually."

"Eventually." Sully threw up his hands and turned his back to his father. "Did you hear that, Fe? He was *eventually* going to see me. Do you know what?" He was furious when he turned back around. "Ofelia's father is in a hospital, and he goes out of his way for her ten times more than you do for me."

Zeke did the one thing Ofelia wasn't expecting and rolled his eyes. "Oh, don't be dramatic, Zach. I came for you the second I realized you were in trouble. Give me a break. You're such a drama queen."

"Yeah, insult him," Ofelia drawled. "That will help."

"You're a drama queen too," Zeke said to her. "Together, you're the drama king and queen of the French Quarter.

Although ... I just said you were both drama queens. I guess that makes you the twin queens of drama."

"Well, I'm glad we got that distinction out of the way," Ofelia fired back. She wasn't glad about any of this in the least. "Now tell me what's going on with those mimes."

"I have no idea." Zeke held his hands palms out. "I just ... don't know. They're stalking me for some unknown reason."

"Oh, he's lying," Sully protested. "He knows what they want. I'm sure he did something to someone to cause this to happen. You're the reason those people are dead."

Ofelia reached out a tentative hand with the intention of wrapping her fingers around Sully's wrist to offer him some support. He pulled away from her before she could.

"Let's go," Sully barked.

Ofelia was understandably surprised. "Go where?"

"Away from him." Sully waved his hand toward his father. "We're not staying here. He's a liar, and he's about to drag us into his problems. I'm not putting up with it. We're going." He waved his hand again.

Ofelia eyed it for a beat, debating, and then shook her head. "I think we need to talk to him."

"I don't want to talk to him."

Ofelia wasn't used to Sully being the irrational one in their relationship. He almost never melted down. Unfortunately, there was very little she could do for him right now. "Zach, we need to get the information on why these mimes are chasing him from your father. We can't just ignore the situation."

He stared at her a beat, incredulous, and then turned on his heel before stomping off in the direction of home.

Ofelia watched him for several seconds, and when she turned back to Zeke, she was at the end of her rope. "I'm going to be honest with you," she said. "I have not liked you from the moment I laid eyes on you. I felt something was off, and I was obviously right."

"Do you want applause?" Zeke queried.

Ofelia ignored him. "You're going to tell me what's going on. You're going to do it without being a douche. When you're done, you're going to go back to your hotel, and I'm going to have a talk with Zach. Then, tomorrow, we're going to come up with a solution."

"And what if I say no?"

"Then I will make it so you never get an erection again. I'll curse the hell out of you and your little friend."

Zeke only hesitated for a moment. "That's a very effective threat. Okay, I'll talk. You're not going to like it, though."

Ofelia wasn't even marginally surprised at that news. "Somehow, I knew you were going to say that."

# 11

## ELEVEN

"I have a business deal that's sort of gone south," Zeke explained. "It started out fine—everything was going really well actually—and then I realized that the property we were supposed to build on wasn't going to work because some environmentalists were going to try and stop me from putting up a high-rise. They claimed there was some rare bird there that needed its nesting ground protected. Like that's a thing."

Ofelia narrowed her eyes. "What bastards," she drawled.

"Right?" Zeke started fluttering his hands.

"I was talking about you," Ofelia growled. Something occurred to her. "I thought you were in the oil business."

"I am." Zeke's smile fled in an instant. "Let me guess, Zach told you that I was in the oil business when you asked."

"Is that not true?"

"It's a gross underestimation of my business prowess." Zeke puffed out his chest. "I am in many businesses. Oil is just one of them."

"Do that again, and I'll deflate you like a balloon," Ofelia warned. She sat down on the bench next to him and debated how to proceed. "Who is this business deal with?"

"An industrial group. I'm not sure the specifics are important."

"They are if you want us to fix this," Ofelia shot back. Her frustration was palpable. "Those mimes have targeted you, and they're deadly. We need to know who conjured them so we can end this."

"Can't you just kill the mimes?"

"Sure, but what's to stop this individual from conjuring more? We don't even know if a spell was cast to call existing mimes, or if they were created from out of nowhere, or random people were taken over and forced to be mimes."

Zeke looked horrified at the thought. "You don't think that's what's happening, do you?"

"Probably not. I'm guessing they were conjured out of nowhere. We don't know, though. That's the point."

There was no mirth on Zeke's face when Ofelia looked up again.

"You know what the worst thing about this is," she said in a low voice. "It's that you came to New Orleans and weren't even going to see your son." She found she was disgusted at the prospect when she stood. "You make me mad, Zeke."

"I was fairly certain you already hated me," he noted. "How much worse can it possibly be now that you know the truth?"

"It's bad, Zeke. My mother is in what I'm convinced is a racist power-walking group and yet you're somehow worse. That should be a lesson to you."

Zeke let loose a groan. "What do you want me to do?"

"Well, for starters, I'm going to walk you back to your hotel. Where are you staying?"

"The Royal Sonesta."

That irritated Ofelia more than she was expecting. "So a block and a half from where your son lives and you weren't going to see him."

"I didn't say I wasn't going to see him," Zeke fired back.

Ofelia folded her arms over her chest and waited.

"I was going to call him and say I had an overnight business trip and meet him for drinks on my last night."

"Oh, how magnanimous of you." Ofelia wanted to smack him. The urge was almost overwhelming. To her surprise, she leaned over and hit him. It wasn't a slap either. It was a punch. It was hard enough to cause his head to snap back. They both looked surprised when she pulled back.

"Ow!" Zeke rubbed his cheek. "What was that for?"

"You suck." Ofelia got to her feet. She was mad, and punching Zeke had made her feel better. Normally, she wasn't someone to embrace violence. He deserved it, though.

"I happen to think I'm a good father."

"My father is mentally ill, and he's ten times the father you are," Ofelia shot back. "Heck, my mother walks around with racists trying to find homeless people to call the police on, and she's better than you. I mean ... what is wrong with you?"

"I think you've had attitude about me since the moment we met, and that's not fair."

"I don't really care what you think is fair," Ofelia shot back. "Honestly, you're just the absolute worst."

Zeke rubbed his cheek for a few more seconds and then

dropped his hand. "What do you want from me? Are you going to do nothing and let them kill me?"

"Did I say I was going to do nothing?"

"No, but ... you obviously don't like me."

"I don't like the way you disrespect your son. He's the best man I've ever met."

Zeke rolled his eyes. "Geez. You guys are like high school sweethearts, you're so sappy."

"No, we're adults who stand with each other no matter what. You're the child in this scenario. A big, stupid child."

"How are you going to fix this?"

"I like how you assume it should just fall on me to fix."

"You're the one who said that you weren't going to abandon me," he pointed out.

Ofelia stared at him a beat longer, imagined all the ways she could force him to be quiet for the foreseeable future, and then sighed. "Meet us at the Stanley at nine o'clock tomorrow for breakfast. Bring all the information on who you're fighting with to the meeting."

Zeke blinked several times in rapid succession. "That's it?"

"For now."

"What are you going to do? Are you going to hunt the mimes?"

"The mimes aren't going to be found if they don't want to be found," Ofelia replied. "Right now, they're trying to figure out how to deal with me. That means I need to get you back to your hotel, and then I need to find your son."

"How do you know they won't track you to kill you?"

"Because I'm stronger than them, and they know it. They're going to try to ambush me and take me out. It's not happening tonight, though. Tonight, I need to find your son and deal with him."

"He's always been a moody little thing," Zeke agreed.

Ofelia murdered him with a glare.

"He's also been a great son," Zeke added. "Just ... the absolute best."

"I so want to punch you again," Ofelia growled. "Just ... come on." She motioned for him to follow her. "I'll drop you off, but you have to stay in that hotel for the rest of the night. That means no going anywhere, including the bar."

"You're very strict," Zeke complained as he fell into step behind her. "Why do you think that is? Do you take after your mother? You do, don't you?"

"Shut it. I'm done talking to you."

"Fine. I'm not done talking to you, though. I'm going to yammer the whole way back to the hotel."

"Honestly, I would expect nothing less from you."

"I am wonderfully predictable ... and extremely handsome. You can thank me for my son's good looks."

"Stop talking!"

"Yeah, I think I'm good."


**OFELIA WAS FRUSTRATED TO THE POINT** of no return when she got home. She checked in with the Krewe staff, found things were running smoothly, and then headed upstairs. She expected to find Sully on the couch, maybe kicked back with a beer in his hand and the cat in his lap. Instead, she found the clothes Sully had been wearing in a heap in the middle of the living room.

She took a moment to consider what could have possibly happened—was he so steaming mad he had to strip to cool off?—and then she moved toward the bedroom. Her search came up empty. He wasn't in the bathroom either.

On a whim, she stepped out onto the patio. She'd never known Sully to run around naked out there, but perhaps that was his mood. She didn't immediately find him. He wasn't in his favorite spot on the wicker couch. He wasn't standing next to the grill with tongs and a smile. He was nowhere to be found.

A hint of movement to her left caught her attention, and she prepared herself for a mime attack. Instead, one building over, a sleek majestic panther prowled the rooftop garden. Even from a distance she could see how glossy his fur looked. It made her want to pet him, and not in a sexy way. Although, now that she thought about it, that wasn't out of the question.

She opened her mouth to call to him before thinking better of it. Instead, she moved to the couch and sat. If Sully needed to shift and roam to get his aggression out, she couldn't get in the way of that. Sure, it was something she'd never seen him do before, but that didn't mean he was wrong to do it.

After a few minutes, her restless energy got the better of her, so she headed inside. She changed into comfortable sleep pants and a tank top. She mixed herself a violet gin and tonic. She pulled her hair back, washed her face, and then returned to the patio. By the time she sat, Sully was on a different rooftop. She watched him wander around a pool in the distance, pursed her lips when he plunged into the pool in his panther form, and then focused on her phone.

It was rare that Ofelia had time to play games, but she needed to be patient now, so she pulled up her card game app and settled in.

It was almost an hour before Sully returned. She heard him land on the patio steps before she turned to look for him, and she got a rare treat when he stretched his sinewy muscles and didn't immediately turn back into his human form.

"Hello, handsome," she drawled.

The panther padded over to her and sat to her right. Carefully, she extended her hand to stroke the top of his head.

"I have no idea if this is okay," she admitted. "We've never really talked about panther shifter etiquette. You rarely shift around me, and I kind of got used to that. It's come to my attention this evening, however, that maybe I've done you a disservice."

He made a chuffing sound, and his glare was obvious.

"I'm being serious," Ofelia said. "You're very pretty like this." She touched his ears and was surprised when he started purring. "Oh, good grief, that is amazing." She leaned close so she could better hear the sound, pressing her ear to his chest area. "I kind of want to take you to bed like this."

Sully picked that moment to shift, making sure to catch her so she didn't hit the ground when the cat disappeared, and the man took his place.

"That was way too much," he announced as he stared into her eyes.

She grinned at him, breathless. "You're naked."

"Oh, so it's not *all* nudity you're opposed to," he teased as he settled her on the couch. "It's just my father's nudity."

"Pretty much," she agreed.

He left her there long enough to snag the boxer shorts he'd shed right before he shifted. They were separate from his other clothes. Then he plopped down next to her on the couch. "Did you miss me?"

Ofelia didn't have to ask what he was doing. It was obvious. He was deflecting.

"I always miss you," she replied. "I am curious about something, though." When he didn't speak, she took that as her opportunity to continue. "Do you do this often and just not tell me?"

"Do I do what?" Sully picked up her feet, placed them in his lap, and started rubbing. He needed something to do with his hands.

"Do you roam the various rooftops in this area in your panther form?"

He shrugged. He wasn't meeting her steady gaze right now. "I don't know. Why? Is it important?"

"Yeah, it's important."

"I might do it occasionally." Sully hadn't realized how uncomfortable he was talking about shifter stuff with her until this very moment. "Sometimes I do it when you're working a late shift. It's not a big deal."

"I think it is."

"Why?"

"Because you wait until I'm not around to do it, which proves you're not comfortable with me."

Sully balked. "That is a gross exaggeration. I never said anything of the sort."

"You don't have to say it. I finally see it." She refused to take her eyes off him. She understood, intrinsically, that this was a very important conversation. "I want you to be yourself. If this is what you want to do, or *need* to do, then I want you to do it. We'll carve out time whenever we can for it."

"It's not that." Anguished annoyance rode roughshod over Sully's features. "It's just ... well ... when I am frustrated, I need to shift. I haven't been frustrated much since meeting you. Tonight, this wasn't about you. This was about him."

Ofelia didn't have to ask who the "him" in question was. "You haven't been frustrated with me the entire time we've been together?" she challenged. "Forgive me if I call bull on that statement. We've fought. I've been a baby when it comes to my father and brother. You've definitely been frustrated."

"It's different," he countered. "My father knows how to press every button I have. Every single button. I revert to my reactions when I was a teenager and needed to shift constantly to vent my aggression whenever he's around."

Ofelia understood what he was saying. Well, mostly. "You can shift with me," she prodded. "When I'm here, you can shift and do whatever you want to do. You don't have to wait until I'm at work. I don't want you suppressing such a big part of yourself. It's not going to make for a very healthy relationship going forward."

"I'm not suppressing myself," he assured her. "That's not what this is. I just ... I don't know. When we're together, I'm always happy and content. Even when we're in the middle of a case, I don't feel the need to shift because my nerves are never frayed."

"I still want you to do it," Ofelia insisted. "I think it's important."

"So, you want to force me to shift whether I want to do it or not?"

She realized how it sounded, but she didn't back down. "I want you to do what makes you feel best."

A devilish gleam came into his eyes, and she jabbed a finger in his face to stop him in his tracks.

"Not that," she warned. "Not yet. I'm being serious, though. I mean ... what about any future kids we have?"

The question caught Sully off guard. "What about them?" he asked finally.

"Will they be able to shift?"

"I don't know." He held out his hands. "With hybrid children, it's not always a given that they will be able to shift. Our children will be doubly special because of your witchy genes. Basically, we won't know what we're getting until they reach the age where they would normally shift."

"Which is when?"

"Twelve."

Ofelia nodded. "And our kids might be even later than that because they'll be half and half."

"Pretty much." Sully dug his fingers into her arch and made her moan. His flirty smile was back, although tension lined his eyes. "How did you leave things with my father?"

"Before or after I punched him?"

Sully's eyebrows hopped. "You punched him?"

"He was bugging me."

"I guess that means we're leaving him to his own devices. That's good. That's smart." Despite saying it, Ofelia could tell he was conflicted if he actually believed it.

"Yeah, not so much." Ofelia saw no reason to hold back. "I told him he was the absolute worst—and he is—but we're meeting him for breakfast at the Stanley tomorrow."

Sully started shaking his head before she was finished speaking. "No, we're not."

"Yes, we are." Ofelia was taking control, and that meant Sully had no choice but to hold on for the ride. "We can't just abandon him. He swears it has something to do with some business deal he's involved in. I didn't get the specifics because I was too irritated. He'll give them to us tomorrow."

"I don't want the specifics," Sully growled. "I don't want any of this."

"Then you don't have to deal with him." Ofelia opted to give him a way out. "I'll deal with him. It's fine."

A muscle worked in Sully's jaw. "I don't want you to work with him either," he said finally. "He did this. I'm sure he did something underhanded because that's what he does. I think we should leave him to clean up his own mess."

"Normally, I wouldn't have a problem with that, but you're going to blame yourself for not helping if something happens, so we can't do that. If you can't bring yourself to help him, I get it. He seems like a complete and total tool. I'll handle it."

"Oh, right," Sully muttered. "Like I'm just going to sit back and let you help my father and do nothing. That sounds just like me."

Ofelia softened her voice. "We can't do nothing, Zach. We have to do something."

"I know. I just ... he makes me angry."

"He's a jerk, but we don't have a choice in the matter. Those mimes killed three innocent people. We still don't know why. We can't just sit back and leave him to his own devices because he's not going to do what needs to be done."

Sully considered it for several seconds, then nodded. "You're right. We have to protect the people of this city. My father has put them in danger. Just because we're going to help, though, that doesn't mean I have to be nice to him."

"I actually think you should tell him exactly what you're feeling," Ofelia said. "He's earned it."

"Yeah." Sully shifted, so he was next to her and pulled her tight, resting his chin on her shoulder. "Just out of curiosity, how did it feel to punch him?"

"Really good. I would recommend doing it if the impulse arises."

"Did he cry?"

"No, but he wanted to. I'm sure he would cry if you did it."

"That's something to think about." Sully brushed his lips against her cheek. "Are we done talking about the serious stuff?"

"I don't know. I guess that depends. What did you have in mind?"

"I thought we could roll around on the ground and get sweaty."

"Out here?"

"Do you have a problem with that?"

Ofelia only considered it for a few seconds. "Nope. Does shifting like you did give you energy for the fun stuff?"

Sully grinned and rolled her to the ground. "Let's find out, shall we?"

# 12

## TWELVE

Ofelia was feeling surprisingly spry the next morning. She figured her back would hurt from all the rolling around—she and Sully were outside for hours—but there were no aches and pains to tug on her regret.

She headed straight for the shower upon waking and finding the other side of the bed empty. By the time she made it to the kitchen, after tying her hair up on either side of her head in low, loose buns, she was ready for a huge meal. She found Sully in the kitchen drinking coffee, Baron at his feet chowing down on the tuna Sully had given him, and she raised an eyebrow as she poured her own coffee.

"Are you regretting last night?" she asked.

"Which part?" He managed a small smile. "If you're asking if I regret what we did on the patio, that's a big, fat no."

She lightly flicked his ear as she walked past so she could grab the flavored creamer from the refrigerator. "That is not what I was talking about."

"Then what were you talking about?" Sully made a face

when she dropped half a cup of salted caramel creamer in her mug. "Why not just snort the sugar?"

Ofelia ignored him and waited.

"If you're asking if I regret agreeing to help my father, the answer is no."

She smiled. "Good."

"I'm going to be snarky and mean to him, though," he added.

"I'm fine with that." She meant it. "Just out of curiosity, are you really okay going to a family counseling session with my father? I know you said you were last night, but I figured you were just saying that because you wanted to keep the conversation going."

"I wasn't just saying that. I meant it. I think we should definitely do the family counseling session."

"Thank you." Ofelia's heart squeezed. "If you need to shift and wander around on top of buildings after, I completely understand. I'm grateful though."

Sully pinned her with a dark look. "I don't like when you say things like that. Your father is part of my family now. You don't have to be grateful."

"And your father is part of mine," she said pointedly. "We're going to have to deal with this as a family even though you don't want to do it. You realize that, right?"

Sully hesitated, but only for a moment. "I realize that. My father is going to have to listen to some hard truths from me for a change. Mostly I let him slide because I rarely see him, and what's the point? I'm not doing that any longer, though. He has to get it together."

"I think that's more than fair." Ofelia rolled up to the balls of her feet, so she was at even eye level with him before planting a loud kiss on the corner of his mouth. "Have I mentioned I love you?" she whispered.

He grinned at the flirty intent in her eyes. "Not today, but it's always nice to hear. I love you too. In fact, if you're feeling lovey-dovey—which you clearly are—we could take this party right back to the bedroom."

Ofelia shot him a "not gonna happen" look. "We have to be at the Stanley in fifteen minutes. That means we have to essentially leave now. There's no time to go to the bedroom."

"We could be late for breakfast with my father. He's earned it."

"I think it's best that we figure out what we're dealing with." Ofelia gave him another kiss before heading to the mat by the door to collect her shoes. "We can play under-the-covers games to your heart's content when we're done."

"Fine." Sully finished his coffee and then moved the mug into the sink. "You realize my father is going to be an absolute tool, right? Like ... even more than normal."

"Because he feels vulnerable? Yeah. I've figured that out."

"I just want to prepare you."

"I'm Marie Charles's daughter," she reminded him. "I can handle a passive aggressive parent who hides insults behind compliments. I'm not a novice."

That elicited a smile from him. "I'm kind of looking forward to seeing what you do to him."

"You should. I'm going to be an absolute delight."

"Good. I like it when you're mean."

"Then you're about to fall in love with me all over again."

"Be still my beating heart."

. . .

**ZEKE WAS ALREADY AT A TABLE WHEN THEY** arrived at the Stanley.

"You're late," he noted in pouty fashion as he sipped his coffee.

Ofelia ignored him and immediately snagged a menu as the server crossed to them. "I want the corned beef hash but with eggs over medium," she said. "I'll also take a glass of tomato juice and a glass of water."

Zeke made a face. "Tomato juice? Really?"

Sully pinned his father with a warning look before placing his order. "I'll have the Stanley Classic with scrambled eggs, but I'll take the corned beef hash instead of the grits. I'll have a glass of grapefruit juice and some coffee too." He smiled at the server for good measure.

"I guess we're not bothering with pleasantries this morning," Zeke complained. "I'll have the Breakfast Seafood Platter," he said. "I'll have a glass of grapefruit juice as well."

The server smiled, happy to have things truncated, and collected the menus before taking off.

"So, how was your night?" Zeke asked when she was gone.

"None of your business," Sully replied. "Let's talk about your new enemy."

"I don't know that I would say she's a new enemy," Zeke hedged.

Ofelia sat straighter in her chair. "She?"

"Oh, now you're interested." Zeke bobbed his head, seemingly thrilled that he'd gotten Ofelia's attention. "You like a solid fight, don't you? I bet you don't even pull hair. Given that right cross of yours, you go straight for the eyes, don't you?" He made a tsking sound with his tongue. "That's a bit disappointing given the fact that you would be uber hot if you started gouging out eyes and covering your-self in mud."

"I will break your neck if you say anything like that to her again," Sully warned in an icy voice. He was obviously serious, because after Zeke uncomfortably eyed his son for several seconds, he held up his hands in surrender.

"Sorry," Zeke offered. "I didn't realize you were feeling sensitive this morning."

"There's nothing different about this morning," Sully replied. "I'm so furious with you right now I don't know where to start. Despite that, it's hardly a new feeling where you're concerned. You will, however, stop sexually harassing my fiancée. I'll kill you if you do it again." He issued the threat just as the server arrived with their juice and coffee.

"Ignore him," Ofelia said to the twenty-something woman when she visibly blanched. "It's just father and son stuff."

"Oh." The server let out a shaky breath. "Is that all? I thought it was something serious."

Ofelia took her juice with a smile, then waited for the server to leave before speaking. "You two have got to get it together. This is not acceptable. Like ... at all. You don't have to like each other, but you do have to work together. We have no choice in the matter given what's happening."

"Ah, you're wise *and* beautiful," Zeke drawled. "I can see why my son is head over heels for you."

"Don't push me," Ofelia warned.

On a sigh, Zeke sipped his coffee. He was serious when he spoke again. "I've been working on a deal. It's for a piece of property down the riverbank, over on the west side. It's just a small strip of parkland."

"On the river?" Ofelia queried. She was trying to picture

the area he was talking about but was having trouble. "What parkland is there on the riverbank to the west unless..." Slowly she straightened. "Are you talking about Audubon Park?"

"You've heard of it?" Zeke was all smiles.

"Are you kidding me right now?" Ofelia's temper bubbled close to the surface. "Audubon Park is one of my favorite places to go when the weather is nice."

"Mine too," Sully said. "We should go on a picnic there now that the weather is getting more tolerable."

"We should," Ofelia agreed.

"If the park is still there," Zeke grumbled. He realized he'd said it out loud when it was too late to take it back and straightened. "What was I saying again?"

"Nothing good," Sully replied. "Were you really looking to build a high rise on that property?"

"We were only going to use a section of the property," Zeke countered. "There are ballparks there right now. I mean ... ballparks. Who uses ballparks in this day and age?"

"People who like to play ball," Sully snapped. He couldn't believe his father was being so lackadaisical about this. "I love that park. What is the matter with you?"

"It's a good development," Zeke insisted. "It's going to be high-end condos. I was going to suggest you guys move there to get out of the French Quarter. I'll even get you a deal. I mean ... if I'm not dead and the development still happens, which seems like a long shot."

"If I have to curse every single person on the zoning board, I guarantee that development will never happen," Ofelia promised. "It's done. Dead in the water. You're going to be dead in the water too if you don't start talking."

"I was getting there." Zeke made an impatient face. "You have the patience of a toddler, young lady."

"You're going to see how my patience feels firmly shoved up your behind if you're not careful," Ofelia hissed.

Sully gave her an appraising look. "I'm so turned on watching you threaten my father right now. It's amazing."

Ofelia preened as she stared back at him. "Thank you, baby."

"You're welcome." He leaned in and gave her a cute kiss. When he looked up, he found his father scowling at them. "Get used to it," he said. "We're going to keep doing this until the day we die. And, because we plan to be cutesy even in death, we're going to die together so nobody has to live without the other one."

"Aw." Ofelia went warm all over as she leaned her head against his shoulder. "That is the sweetest thing I've ever heard."

"I thought you would like it."

"Oh, my God, shoot me now," Zeke complained.

"I can make that happen," Sully warned, returning to business. "Tell me why you think it was this development that caused the mimes to be unleashed."

"Because that development is all I've been working on for the past four months," Zeke replied. He was deadly serious now. "I thought we had the park land secured. The plan was to have everything sewed up, neat and tidy like, before news even broke that it was going to happen. Somehow an environmental group found out, though, and they filed an injunction based on some rare bird living out there. Some sort of grackle. Before I knew it, the development was not just temporarily off the rails but dead forever."

Sully made a snorting noise. "What a bummer for you, huh?"

"It was a bummer. I had a million of my own dollars

tied up in the work that we'd been doing. I figured it would be fine because I would make thirty times that when the building was finished. Guess what, though? The building isn't going to be finished, and that money is gone."

"I don't feel sorry for you," Sully argued.

"Me either," Ofelia agreed.

"Hey, the money I lost was nothing compared to what my partner lost," Zeke said. "She lost twenty times that ... and she's mad. She wants her money back. I told her no, that these things happen, and she's going to have to suck it up, and that's when the stuff started happening."

"Here we go." Sully rubbed his hands under the table. "What sort of stuff?"

"Well, for starters, I started seeing people smiling as they walked past me on the sidewalk. It wasn't just smiles either. It was these creepy 'I'm a killer clown in my spare time' smiles. Still, I smiled back. It didn't occur to me that it could be something I should be afraid of."

"But you changed your mind at some point," Ofelia guessed.

He nodded. "Your mother had an event in Baton Rouge a few days ago," he explained to his son. "It was one of those big charity events. You know how tedious they are."

"You signed up for them," Sully argued. "You knew what sort of life she wanted when you married her." There was warning in his voice. He was telling his father that if he talked badly about his mother, things wouldn't go well.

"Chill out," Zeke muttered. "I wasn't being mean. I was just setting the stage for what happened."

"Uh-huh." Sully clearly wasn't convinced.

"I was at the bar having a few drinks to numb the tedium when the bartender started smiling at me the same way the people on the street did," he said. "It was terrifying.

One minute he'd been gregarious and cracking jokes. The next he was smiling at me as if he was going to eat me. He wasn't the same person."

"That's what the old lady in the apartment next door to the one where the bodies were found said," Ofelia mused.

Sully nodded, his hand finding her knee under the table. He didn't say anything. He just waited for his father to continue.

"I knew there was something wrong," Zeke explained. "It had been three days of really weird smiles. We're talking nightmare-inducing smiles. I was still shocked when he broke a liquor bottle and jammed it in his own throat."

Ofelia straightened. "He did what?"

"You heard me." Zeke made a disgruntled sound under his breath. "I just stood there like a moron. I couldn't believe what was happening. Some people started screaming for a doctor. I was about to call 911. That's when the mimes paraded into the room, though."

"And what did you do?" Sully demanded.

"Hey, I'm not an idiot," Zeke fired back. "If you think I'm going to stick around and keep watching when things go off the rails, you're wrong. I did the smart thing and left."

"Did you take my mother with you?" Sully practically exploded.

"No, but she was hanging out with ten other people. She was fine."

"No, you knew you were the target and couldn't risk anybody seeing you make a run for it," Ofelia countered. She was just as disgusted as Sully. "What is the matter with you?"

"I did what was right for myself and left," Zeke replied. "I tried to call Celeste—I knew it was her—but she didn't answer. That's why I decided to come here and make things right. I thought maybe I could get the development back on track. It doesn't look like that is possible, though."

Sully slid his eyes to Ofelia. There was so much he wanted to say that he didn't know where to start. Ofelia was the one to take control.

"Who is Celeste?" she demanded.

"Celeste Cunningham," he replied. "She's head of Ponchatrain Industrial. Until recently, I'd thought she was one of my best development partners. Obviously, I was wrong on that front."

"Have you heard of her?" Sully asked Ofelia when she didn't immediately respond.

She nodded. "I've heard of her. She's a witch. At least I think she is. She was part of Dora's coven at one time. Dora cut her loose, though."

"Why would she do that?" Sully asked. As far as he knew, the Frenchman Street witch never did anything without a reason.

"The rumor was that Celeste thought a change in management was in order," Ofelia replied. "I'm sure you can guess who she wanted to take over. Dora isn't letting that coven go until she's dead, so it was a battle of wills."

"Obviously, Dora won," Sully noted.

Ofelia bobbed her head. "Yeah, but I heard that Celeste took a few of Dora's most prized witches with her when she left." She was annoyed when she fixed her gaze on Zeke. "Did you ever see the same few women hanging around with Celeste?"

"Now that you mention it, I did," Zeke confirmed. "She always has the same two hanging around. A blonde and a brunette. They're both sexy as hell and wear these tight little librarian skirts that make me want to check out endless romance novels for inspiration."

"You're gross," Ofelia muttered. "Just ... so, so gross."

"He's all talk," Sully countered. "He runs his mouth about other women, but he's really terrified by my mother and wouldn't risk cheating on her lest she find out. She would take too much of his money if she divorced him."

"I love your mother," Zeke shot back. "I would never cheat on her."

"You fear my mother," Sully corrected. "There's a difference. Although ... I do believe part of you loves my mother. You're still an unbelievable tool, though."

"Yeah, yeah, yeah." Zeke waved his hand. "If you know Celeste, does that mean you can take her out? That would be a real lifesaver."

The question was directed at Ofelia, so she was the one who answered. "I know her in a very vague sense. We've only crossed paths at a few of my mother's events. On the witchy front, we've been kept separate. I'm not going to kill her until I know for certain she's involved."

"Oh, it's her," Zeke insisted. "You can take my word for it."

Ofelia ignored him. "I can go over and see her," she said to Sully. "She's got an office in the Warehouse District."

"And you can kill her there," Zeke volunteered. "That's smart."

Sully pointed at his father to silence him but kept his eyes on Ofelia. "Do you want me to go with you?"

"Actually, I think that's the worst possible move," she replied. "You have a badge, and it will come across as aggressive. I need to do it myself."

"I don't know if I'm okay with that," Sully hedged. "Will you be safe?"

"She's not going to start throwing around magic in her building, in front of all her employees," Ofelia replied. "She knows that wouldn't go over well. She'll hear me out. Then, if she deems me a threat, she'll send the mimes after me."

"I'm not sure I like that idea any better than her moving on you now," Sully argued.

"We can't do nothing." Ofelia opted to be pragmatic. "We have to make a move. This is the only one I can think of."

Because he didn't disagree, Sully nodded. "Fine, but I want you to check in with me before and after your conversation. I want to keep tabs on you … just in case."

Ofelia nodded. "Just in case," she agreed.

"What about me?" Zeke queried. "What do you want me to do?"

"I want you to not make things worse," Sully replied. "Do you think you can manage that?"

"I have no idea. There's always a first time for everything, though, right?"

"There had better be. I'm not in the mood for your crap."

"I'll be an absolute angel," Zeke promised. "You won't even know I'm in town."

"Won't that be a nice change of pace?"

# 13
## THIRTEEN

Ofelia didn't go to the Warehouse District often. It wasn't because she didn't like the Warehouse District—honestly, it had some great restaurants —but she was a French Quarter girl at heart. She'd been raised there. She loved the vibe. The Warehouse District simply didn't have the same vibe.

When she was outside of Celeste's building, which was located on Julia Street, she pulled her phone out to call Sully. She had promised she would check in, and she meant it.

He answered on the first ring.

"You'd help me hide a body, right?" he queried by way of greeting. He sounded out of breath and annoyed. "You love me that much, don't you?"

Ofelia laughed. "Sure. Who are we burying?"

"Who do you think?"

Ofelia didn't bother to say his father's name. "He's an ass. Just ignore him."

"I'm starting to think he's purposely an ass."

Ofelia had come to the same conclusion too. "That's totally possible."

Sully sighed, and Ofelia could picture him sucking in a deep breath to center himself. "Are you about to go in?" he asked when he was finished.

"I am," she confirmed. "I'm on the street. I was thinking, though. When this is over with, we should come out here for dinner. They have some restaurants I wouldn't mind visiting. We always go to the same places."

She was buying time. Sully likely knew that. He indulged her all the same. "What restaurants are we talking about?"

"Well, for starters, they have Pêche Seafood."

"Is that the one where they put the full fish on your plate?" Sully didn't sound impressed. "Like ... they leave the head on and everything."

"Yes, but I'm sure they would cut the head off if you ask."

"I don't want to eat anything when it's looking back at me. It freaks me out."

"They have Emeril's over here, too," Ofelia argued.

"Isn't that the one that forces you into a three-course meal and doesn't allow you to eat what you want?"

She was starting to get exasperated. "What about Galliano? They have Cajun Wellington, and it makes me feel romantic."

"See, baby, you could've just led with that," Sully drawled. "Their food is good, though. I seem to remember that they have an Alligator Creole over there that changed my life. Oh, and they have a really good pork chop. I know that a pork chop sounds mundane, but theirs is stuffed and grilled, and it's amazing."

Ofelia stared at nothing for a moment. Then she burst

out laughing. "How did you know that talking about food would settle my nerves?"

"Because I've met you. If you want to meet over there for dinner, though, they have an amazing seafood stew, too."

"I don't plan on being over here that long," Ofelia assured him. "However, once this is over with and your father is out of our hair, I would totally be up for a romantic meal in this area of town."

"You had me at romantic, Fe." He was quiet a beat. "Do you want to change your mind? I can tell that you're nervous. If you want to wait, I can be over there in fifteen minutes."

Ofelia was already shaking her head, even though he couldn't see it, before he finished. "No, it's better if I do this alone. I need to feel her out. If you're there, as an official presence, it's going to put her back up. It's better to see how she reacts with just me. If we have to go there, we will. We don't have to go there just yet, though."

"I get it. I don't particularly like you putting yourself in danger because of something my father did, but I get it. Just be careful."

"I will. Try not to kill your father."

"No promises. He's making a bunch of noise about wanting to watch me on the job. It's beyond frustrating."

"Why would he want to watch you on the job?"

"Because he's so proud."

Ofelia made a face. She was certain that Sully was making the same face on the other end of the call. "He's really the worst. I'm going to beat him up again before this is all said and done."

"I'm going to help you."

She was silent a beat. "I should get this over with. I'll call you when I'm finished."

"If you take more than forty-five minutes, I'm sending uniforms over there. Make sure she knows I'm aware of your location and that I'll send in the cavalry if you go missing."

"Yes, because that won't be awkward or anything."

"Just make sure she knows. I don't trust her, and it's not just because she worked with my father."

"I get it. I'll make sure she knows."

"Then I'll see you soon."

"You will. Don't worry."

"I can't help myself. The mimes are creepy."

"Yeah. Only a deranged mind would think of them."

**CELESTE'S OFFICE WAS ON THE THIRD FLOOR OF** the building, so that's where Ofelia pointed herself. There was a reception desk directly in front of her when she exited the elevator, and when Ofelia introduced herself and said she wanted to talk to Celeste, she expected pushback. Instead, she was ushered to the main office on the floor without delay.

"She's expecting you," the receptionist said evenly.

Ofelia stilled, caught between surprise and resignation. Ultimately, she nodded. "Okay, well ... I guess that makes sense." She smoothed the front of her simple V-neck as she made her way down the hallway and paused at the open door she found there.

She was cautious when poking her head inside.

Celeste, hair that could've been blonde or gray tucked neatly behind her ears, glanced up from whatever she was working on. "Have a seat, Ofelia." She sounded indifferent.

Ofelia pressed her lips together. If she wanted to run, now was the time. Running wouldn't get her anywhere, however. What she'd said to Sully had been true. She had no choice but to deal with Celeste now, because dealing with her later wouldn't be an option.

"Close the door," Celeste said to her when she took a step into the office. "I don't think we need everybody knowing our business, do we?"

Ofelia shook her head as she recovered her poise. "Probably not." She shut the door and then sat. It was time to get to the heart of matters. There was no point playing coy. "Why is it that you seem to be expecting me?"

"Because I figured that Zeke would run to you when he realized his time was up," Celeste replied. "He had no love for your witchy ways when he first found out you were dating his son. Now that I'm going to kill him, suddenly you're his best friend. It's so … Zeke." She made a face.

Ofelia had to give the woman credit. She didn't hold back. She liked a blunt woman … even if she was afraid that Celeste's boldness meant that she actually might try to take her out in the middle of the Warehouse District under the bright light of day after all. "You're not even going to bother to deny it, huh?"

"What's the point in that?" Celeste closed the laptop she'd been working on and steepled her fingers as she rested her elbows on the table. "I'm familiar with your reputation. I figured that Zeke would run straight to you when he got into town. I wasn't disappointed."

"He didn't run straight to us, though," Ofelia pointed out. "He tried to deal with you himself. Well, at least that's what I'm guessing. Believe it or not, he hasn't been all that forthcoming with information."

"Oh, I believe it." Celeste made a face. "Honestly, he's

the king of the idiots. They should give him a crown. It would have to be made out of plastic and missing half the jewels, but it would fit him."

"I have to ask, did you really think that you were somehow going to get your hands on Audubon Park property so you could build a high-rise?"

"I too was skeptical," Celeste admitted. "All the paperwork was in place, though. The funds were there. The deal just needed to be punched home. I stood to make a killing ... and then it fell apart."

"Because of the environmentalists."

"Yes, but they're not really the problem," Celeste countered. "I mean ... they are. I would prefer it if they'd curl into balls on the floor and die. They're not going to do that, though."

"No," Ofelia agreed. "They're not."

"Zeke didn't do what he promised to do," Celeste continued. "He didn't cover all his bases. He told me the opposite. He told me we were completely safe. So, guess what happened?"

"You invested twenty million bucks, and now it's going away," Ofelia replied, not missing a beat.

It was impossible to miss the surprise that registered on Celeste's features. "He told you." It wasn't a question.

"He didn't really have a choice. If he wanted help, he had to tell us the truth."

"I didn't even know he recognized the truth. He's not a good man. He lies all the time."

"I get that," Ofelia assured her. "No, really, I do. The thing is, I can't let you kill him despite the fact that he's a big, fat liar."

"Because of your boyfriend?"

"We're getting married." Why that was important was

beyond Ofelia. It was a distinction that needed to be made, though. At least to her. "That means Zeke is going to be my father-in-law."

"Not if you let me kill him." Celeste flashed the sort of smile that made Ofelia think of the mimes. It wasn't pretty.

"I can't let you do that." Ofelia was firm. "He's a complete and total pain in the ass—and then some—but I can't just sit back and do nothing as you try to kill him. I think we need to come to some sort of agreement."

"Is that so?" Amusement tipped up the corners of Celeste's lips. She changed topics smoothly. "When I was coming up, there weren't a lot of witches in the Quarter who were the real deal. You know, not playing the game."

Ofelia wasn't certain where she was going with the shift, but she nodded to encourage Celeste to keep talking. It couldn't hurt, she rationalized. It would give her time to think things out, too.

"Dora had been in power for, gosh, a good twenty years at that point," Celeste explained. "I was late to the witch game. I didn't realize it was a thing. I was born with magic, was capable of manipulating people and even hurting them if I didn't get what I wanted, but I didn't really understand why I could do it. By the time I was curious enough to try to figure it out, I was thirty."

Ofelia leaned back in her chair. This felt as if it was going to be a long story.

"Thankfully for me—or maybe unthankfully, who can say?—the French Quarter is a good place to be when you want information on magic," she continued. "I asked around, realized that half the people didn't realize magic was real, and ultimately landed on Dora as a mentor."

"I can see how that would happen," Ofelia encouraged. "Dora is definitely the real deal."

"She is," Celeste agreed. "She's also stingy about who she shares her knowledge with. She tried to hold me back because she knew I was more powerful than her."

While Ofelia could see Dora doing just that, she didn't believe that the Frenchman Street witch was acting out of malice when it came to Celeste. "Was she trying to hold you back, or teach you about balance?" Ofelia challenged. "Because, the way I heard it, you were too big for your britches right from the start, and Dora had to slap you back because you tried to usurp her."

Celeste let loose a delighted snort. "And who told you that?"

"This town is thick with gossip. You know it as well as anybody else."

"Maybe so." Celeste nodded. "Dora was afraid of me. She knew I was more powerful than her. She tried to manipulate me into believing otherwise."

Ofelia cocked her head, considering. "We all have our own sides to the same story," she said finally.

"You don't believe me."

"I believe parts of it," Ofelia replied. "It's not as if Dora is easy to get along with. I've fought with her on more than one occasion. The thing is, if she believes you're not doing something to hurt others or the city, she usually steps back to see what's going to happen. She doesn't get involved. To me, that suggests she thought you were going to do harm to her city."

"Is that what she thought?" There was something dark and dangerous about Celeste's gaze. "You never learned under her tutelage," she said, changing the topic yet again. "Why is that?"

"I was self-taught," Ofelia replied. "I had too much going on to worry about regular lessons. I read a lot, though, between shifts. I practiced. Dora was interested from afar, but she never infringed on what I was doing."

"Do you think she was afraid of you?"

"I think that she was curious, but disconnected from me," Ofelia replied. "She decided to let me develop at my own pace."

"I wonder why she didn't try to destroy you as she did me." Celeste was thoughtful. "Perhaps she didn't realize you were the threat you clearly are until it was too late. At her age, she wouldn't want to poke the bear. Her legacy is all that she has left."

"Her legacy is fully intact," Ofelia replied. "Trust me. She still has enough magic at her disposal to cause real trouble ... and she likes doing it."

"And what do you like?" Celeste shifted on her chair. "You've been an enigma for quite some time. At first, I thought your whole game plan involved flying under the radar so you could take control when nobody was expecting it. You, however, have kept yourself separate from the other covens. Why?"

"Because I don't feel the need to involve myself with a coven," Ofelia replied. "It's just not my thing."

"And the panther shifter? What edge does he give you?"

"He gives me love," Ofelia replied. "That's all I want from him, and that's all I'm ever going to want from him." Now it was her turn to lean forward. "Why are you so convinced I'm looking for a reason to take over the Quarter?"

"Because you're too powerful not to want to be in control," Celeste replied. "I've been watching you for some time, Ofelia. I've been curious about whether or not we would make a good team. I'm still on the fence about that. I will tell you that if you continue to fight to protect Zeke, we're never going to have a chance to find out, because I'm going to have to kill you."

Ofelia blinked several times in rapid succession, convinced she'd misheard the other witch. Then, to both of their surprise, she burst out laughing. "Is that how you beat your opponents into submission?" she asked when she was done laughing. "Do you tell them crap like that?"

Celeste narrowed her eyes to dangerous slits. "You are not going to like what happens if you don't take me seriously," she warned.

"Oh, I know you're dangerous," Ofelia assured her. "I would never pretend otherwise. No harmless individual could think of those mimes. They're freaky by the way."

Celeste preened. "When I was a teenager, I was once felt up by a mime in Jackson Square. It was the only time in my life I was ever truly afraid. He backed me into a corner and proceeded to try to undo my bra."

Ofelia felt wretched. "That is terrible. Did you call the police?"

"I used my magic to explode his penis."

Ofelia cringed. "Well, that taught him a lesson, huh?" She tried to decide how she felt about it. "I guess he had it coming."

"He was the first of many to try to cross me and live to regret it," Celeste replied. "Zeke won't be the last. He will get what's coming to him for betraying me, though."

"You're not going to get your money back either way," Ofelia pointed out. "What good does killing him do?"

"It sends a message that I am not to be messed with," Celeste replied. "The next developer will not screw with me. As for the money, well, I'm not happy. I'm hardly going to be destitute either."

Ofelia held the other witch's gaze for several seconds,

then lifted her hands and shrugged. "I can't let you kill Zeke. Part of me actually wishes I could let you, and that's the truth. He's a jerk. He's still my fiancé's father. I won't let you kill him."

"And who will you put at risk to stop me?" Celeste challenged. "Will you risk your fiancé in the process? Because, let me tell you something, I will have no problem killing him to get to his father."

"If you touch Zach, I'll make you wish you were never born," Ofelia warned. "The same goes for his father. Just let it go."

"No."

"Then I guess that means we're going to fight." Ofelia was resigned when she got to her feet. "Thanks for seeing me. I was hoping we could talk things out. Obviously not."

"Obviously," Celeste agreed. She didn't stand to show Ofelia out. She looked furious.

"Just out of curiosity, what's the deal with the mimes killing the people in the apartment?" Ofelia queried. "What did those people do to you?"

"Nothing," Celeste replied. "They didn't do anything *for* me either. My children need to eat. Those people weren't doing anything to help the community. They might as well feed my children."

Ofelia felt sick to her stomach. "You don't have to do this," she said.

"I was about to tell you the same thing. I guess it was inevitable that we would face off, though."

"I guess so," Ofelia agreed. "I'll be seeing you around."

"You definitely will."

With that, the meeting was over, and a whole new cauldron of trouble had begun to bubble.

# 14

## FOURTEEN

O felia called Sully when she was leaving Celeste's office.

"Obviously you're still alive," he noted. "Did she act confused about why you were there?"

"Actually, it was the exact opposite." Ofelia filled him in. When she was finished, he was as confused as her.

"So, she's not even pretending she's not responsible for what's happening here?" Sully complained. "Why would she just put it out there like that?"

"I can only think of a few reasons off the top of my head. The biggest is that she's a sociopath and doesn't seem to get that 'normal' people wouldn't admit to anything of the sort. It's also possible she sees me as an extension of Dora."

"But everybody knows you and Dora don't get along," Sully argued. "I knew that even though I only had a vague sense of you before we met."

"You knew what about me?" Ofelia challenged.

"I knew that Dora was frightened of the witch who owned the bar in the French Quarter."

Ofelia made a face. "That could've been anyone."

"Not so much. Your reputation is pretty much carved in stone. I didn't know the real you, but I knew about the witch in the Quarter. It's possible that Celeste feels the same way."

Ofelia considered it for several seconds, then sighed. "I guess that makes sense. All I know is that she's not ashamed of what she's done, and she has no intention of backing down."

"I'm hardly surprised." Sully made a clicking sound with his tongue. "Are you heading over to Frenchman Street?" he asked after several seconds.

"I don't see where I have much of a choice. Dora is going to have the inside scoop on Celeste. I need it."

"Be careful," Sully warned. "You're basically inserting yourself into a war between Dora and Celeste. I don't want you becoming collateral damage."

"I have no interest in becoming collateral damage," Ofelia assured him. "I'll be fine. I've faced way bigger enemies than this."

The words didn't make Sully feel any better. "Just be careful. Losing you isn't an option."

"Weirdly, I feel the same way about you. I'll be fine, though. I don't expect Celeste to make a move right this second. By the way, she thinks your father is a great big turd."

"Almost anybody who has ever met him concurs."

"Just watch him." Ofelia paused a beat. "How are things going with him by the way?"

"How do you think they're going?"

Ofelia didn't have to think too hard. "Just try not to kill him. I'll be in touch after I talk to Dora."

"No promises. I'll do my best, though."

"I guess that's all I can ask."

**DORA LANDRY'S FRENCHMAN STREET MAGIC** shop was the real deal. Compared to the tourist traps situated close to Bourbon Street, Dora's store felt like walking into another world. Dora embraced witchcraft, voodoo, and a few other tenets that Ofelia wasn't completely familiar with. That made Dora strong ... and intimidating.

Over the past few months, Dora had helped Ofelia fight enemies more than once. She'd at least provided information for those fights. That made Ofelia a bit more comfortable when entering Dora's inner sanctum.

They were never going to be best buddies, though.

"I take it you're not here for a social call," Dora drawled when Ofelia slid into the chair next to her. The older witch enjoyed sitting in a rocking chair in front of one of the few working fireplaces in the neighborhood. She emitted an air of strength and old-world charm that enticed shoppers from all over the state. Ofelia didn't have time for the folksy stuff today, though.

"Tell me about Celeste Cunningham," she prodded.

Dora's eyebrows hopped. "Well, that's a blast from the past," she drawled. "Why are you tangling with Celeste?"

"It's not by choice. Trust me. I could've gone my whole life without crossing paths with her and been perfectly happy. She's determined to kill Zach's father, though."

Dora's forehead creased. "Topher Sully?" She looked shocked at the news. "Why?"

"In a nutshell, apparently, he promised her a corner of Audubon Park for a high-rise. He thought he had the deal in the bag. Then some endangered bird was found to have a nesting ground there, and the environmentalists pulled the rug out from under them. She lost like twenty million bucks."

Dora's eyes went wider. "That's quite the nutshell," she said finally.

"Yeah. It's a mess."

"How is she going after him?"

"Magical mimes. The problem is, they're not just sticking to hunting Zeke. I might let them kill him—although probably not really—if he was the only target. The other night, though, they killed three of the Jackson Square folks. They went after Zach to draw in his father the same night. I can't do nothing."

"I heard about the bodies found on Bourbon Street," Dora noted. "I didn't realize that was the mimes."

"Obviously, you've heard about them, too."

"Yeah, but I thought it was just some drunken shenanigans. Maybe a mage killing time. I didn't realize it was magic fueling them."

"According to Celeste—who I just had a lovely meeting with—the mimes have to feed. That's what they were doing on Bourbon Street. She didn't seem apologetic in the least about what she's done."

"Yeah, she wouldn't." Dora wrinkled her nose. "She's a sociopath."

Ofelia nodded. "I kind of figured that out myself."

"She doesn't care about others. The pain of others means absolutely nothing to her."

"Is that why you cut her loose?"

"It was one of the reasons. It wasn't the only reason, though. She thought she could oust me as head of my own coven."

"I've heard stories about that." Ofelia leaned back in her

chair. "People say that she tried to get you to take a subservient position. You declined and sent her packing."

"There's no way that's all that was said."

Ofelia chuckled. "They might've said you pitched an unholy magical fit and beat the crap out of her when you were drumming her out of your coven. This was obviously before my time as a witch. I would've been a child. I didn't get all the good gossip at the time."

"No, you wouldn't have," Dora agreed. "As for Celeste ... she was a late bloomer."

"She said that herself."

"She didn't come into her magic until she was too old. I've rarely seen anyone past the age of twenty-three or so come into their magic and have it end well."

"Why do you think that is?"

"I have a few theories. The strongest is that kids are more malleable. So, when a twelve-year-old realizes she's magical, she adjusts her thinking. Kids can still adjust. You don't think the same way you did when you were twelve."

Ofelia considered it for several seconds, then nodded. "That's true. If I thought the same as when I was twelve, I would be engaged to Zac Efron."

"I have no idea who that is, but good on you ... I guess." Dora made a dubious face. "Anyway, my theory is that your belief system grows more rigid as you age, so if magic comes in when your belief system is already set in stone, things go poorly. Celeste's belief system was carved out of granite when she joined my coven. There was no moving her. She believed she should be in control. That meant she was going to get what she wanted, no matter what."

Ofelia pursed her lips. She could read between the lines easily enough. "She tried to kill you," she realized out loud.

"It wasn't just that she wanted control of the coven. She also wanted to eliminate you."

Dora nodded. "She set a trap. I was ready for it, though. I'd heard the whispers. I saw the discontent on her face whenever I issued an order. I knew she would eventually snap, so I was ready."

"What happened?"

"Let's just say that things didn't go her way." Dora was grim. "I might not be the most popular witch in the Quarter, but the other coven members were smart enough to realize what Celeste's rule would look like. I might've been unpopular, but there's a difference between someone being ... witchy ... and a dictatorship."

Ofelia nodded. "When her attempts failed, she was drummed out. The rumor is that three of your witches went with her."

"Three of my witches were drummed out with her," Dora corrected. "Anyone who sided with her when she attempted to kill me was not allowed to stay. I couldn't keep them around, let them get inside information, and just hope that they wouldn't try again. I had to send a message."

Ofelia stretched her long legs out in front of her. "You could've killed them. You obviously had the power."

"I didn't want to kill them. How would that make me any different from Celeste?"

"And yet you rule with an iron fist."

"Not like she wanted to. I don't want to kill to get my point across."

Ofelia rolled her neck. "I don't know what to do here. I don't particularly like Celeste—in fact, I dislike her a great deal—but I don't like Zeke either."

Rather than ask questions, or commiserate, Dora burst out laughing. "Nobody likes Topher."

Surprise coursed through Ofelia. "You know him?"

"Everybody knows him. At one time or another, he's screwed half the Quarter when trying to wheel his deals. He's not exactly what I would call a good guy."

"Right."

"He's not exactly the Antichrist either," she said. "He's just ... a really obnoxious guy who wants what he wants. It's not as if he's walking around kicking puppies or anything."

"No, but he would evict a single mother and her five kids to get a piece of property he wants."

"Yes, well, nobody said he was a good guy." Dora managed a wan smile. "He's going to be your father-in-law. You can't just let Celeste kill him."

"I know." Ofelia was grouchy when crossing her arms over her chest. "Her mimes are killing people anyway. I can't stand back and allow that."

"What can you tell me about the mimes?"

"I've seen them twice. I managed to shred two of them easily enough the first night, but that was just luck because I was trying to protect Zach at the time. I'm assuming she's bolstering their protections even as we speak."

"She's conjuring them?"

"That was the impression I got."

"Then you should be able to wipe them out. You're stronger than her."

"Yes, but she thinks like an evil monster. I need to get ahead of her. I just don't know how to do it."

"I don't know how you can do it either. You're going to have to be proactive, though. That's the only option you have."

Ofelia didn't disagree. "I'm probably going to have to set a trap."

"Probably."

"Do you think she'll fall for it?"

"There's always a first time for everything."

**OFELIA HAD A LOT TO THINK ABOUT. THERE WAS** no clear-cut path forward. Because she needed to bounce some ideas off someone, she stopped at Pascal's shop on her way home.

"I have a question," Pascal said as he looked up from his *In Touch* magazine. There were two people in the back of his shop, giggling and watching him, but he didn't seem to care.

"I can't handle another conversation about Britney Spears," Ofelia warned.

"Not that." Pascal shook his head. "I need you to explain Scientology to me."

Ofelia made a face. "If I could explain Scientology, I would be rich."

"I've never seen a cult operate out in the open like this," Pascal noted. "I mean ... one of their ambassadors publicly abandoned his own child. The whole thing is pretty sad."

"It *is* pretty sad," Ofelia readily agreed. "I don't care to talk about Scientology right now, though."

"Oh, no?" Pascal lowered the book he was pretending to read, his magazine tucked safely inside. "What do you want to talk about? For the record, if you're here to hire me to kill Topher, I can't help you. The guy is a plague, but I'm not in the mood to hunt him down and snap his neck."

Ofelia shot him a withering look. "I'm not here to

arrange Zeke's death ... although I haven't ruled out killing him myself."

"Zach might thank you if you do."

"No." Ofelia turned sad, her lower lip coming out to play. "He talks big when it comes to his father—to the point where I had no idea that their relationship was so strained —but he still loves him."

"Of course he does. That's his father. He likely feels as if he's being forced to love him against his will."

Ofelia nodded. "I think that's exactly how it feels. He's stretched too thin right now because of his father's presence in our lives. I thought his mother was going to be the worst one. Obviously, I was wrong."

"His mother is a menace on paper. She's an absolute tyrant. The thing is, she never pretends to be something she's not. That's her greatest strength. She is who she is, so he can always rely on her. He might not always like the things she does, but he knows how she's going to react. His father is a different story."

"I don't think Zeke has ever once put his family first," Ofelia admitted. "It's obvious that business comes first for him. His family is just for looks. He probably doesn't even love them."

"I would be careful jumping to that conclusion," Pascal warned. "While Topher is undoubtedly a complete and total pain in the ass, I don't actually doubt that he loves his family."

Ofelia couldn't hide her surprise. "You don't?"

He shook his head. "I don't. I simply think he's limited in how he can show it. That doesn't make him the best man in the world. It doesn't make him the worst man either."

Ofelia considered what he was saying, and then ultimately sighed. "He frustrates me."

"He frustrates you because he frustrates Zach," Pascal countered. "You want to make Zach's life perfect, be there for him because he's been there for you with your father and mother. He doesn't expect you to make things better, though. He understands his father's limitations. The thing that would be better for him is if you just accepted those limitations and didn't push the issue."

Ofelia gave him a dirty look. "I don't push issues."

Pascal snorted.

"I don't," she insisted.

"Why don't we table this conversation for another day, and you tell me what else is going on, huh?" Pascal suggested. "This is a fight that's waiting to happen if we're not careful ... and I don't think either of us wants to risk a fight when there's so much going on at present."

Ofelia didn't disagree. Instead, she nodded. "Well, I know who created the mimes." She told him about Celeste, the meeting they had. She even told him about her conversation with Dora. By the time she was finished, he was nodding and tapping his bottom lip.

"I should've realized that this had Celeste written all over it," he admitted, making a tsking sound with his tongue. "She's always been a wild card."

"I don't know what to do," Ofelia admitted. "Part of me thinks that Zeke should have to deal with this himself. He's not equipped to do it, though. He'll die because he's a moron. All the while, other people will be dying because the mimes are hungry."

"You can't leave it to Topher," Pascal agreed. "He's a complete and total moron. He'll totally foul things up. You're going to have to deal with it yourself."

"Any ideas on how I do that? I'm guessing I'm going to

have to set a trap, although I have no idea when or where to do it."

"Actually, I do have an idea." Pascal's eyes gleamed, causing Ofelia to sit straighter in her chair. "Keep an open mind."

"Oh, see, whenever you say that, I know that things are about to go off the rails," Ofelia lamented.

Pascal chuckled. "It's rare that you get whiny. When you do, you make up for the lack of quantity with an over-abundance of quality, though."

"Just lay it on me."

"There's a charity event tonight. It's over in the Garden District."

Ofelia stilled. "You're talking about the Celestial Cabaret event," she realized out loud.

"I *am* talking about the Celestial Cabaret event," he readily agreed.

Ofelia took a moment to consider it. The event was run by several of the old witches, the ones with influence, and it was meant to help paranormal individuals in need. It wasn't just for witches, but for shifters, mages, vampires, and even sirens. It had been a fixture in New Orleans for more than a hundred years.

"I've never been to the Celestial Cabaret," Ofelia admitted.

"You wouldn't be their cup of tea," Pascal replied. "You have zero old-world sensibilities. You're more of the new age and fabulous variety. They try to avoid that."

"Why should we be focused on that party now?" she asked, legitimately curious.

"Because Celeste will be there. I saw her name on the invitation. She's on the planning committee this year, and that means attendance is mandatory."

"I had no idea." Ofelia tugged on her lower lip, a nervous gesture she'd picked up in childhood. "How are we supposed to get in if we're not invited? It's not like a human party, where we can glamour ourselves and call it a day. They'll stop us at the door."

"I can get invitations."

Ofelia was suddenly suspicious. "How?"

"I make big donations every year. I can do whatever I want."

"But if they see me with you..." Ofelia trailed off.

"It will be fine," Pascal assured her. "They're not going to kick up a fuss with so many people around. They might give me a lecture after the fact, but they won't do anything when people are watching them."

Ofelia nodded. It made an odd sort of sense. "Okay. I'm game. What do we do when we get there, though? Celeste will be suspicious when she sees us."

"You're going to have to decide on that part on your own. I'll help however you want. You're the witch, though. Ultimately, this is your fight. I'm willing to kill as many mimes as necessary. You have to decide how you want this to go down, though."

Ofelia nodded. It made sense. "Okay, well ... I guess I need to talk to Zach. Can you get us more than one extra invitation?"

"How many do you want?"

"At least one other. I wouldn't mind having Angelique with us. Although ... maybe I would be better to try to convince Dora."

"Dora will be there. She always is."

Ofelia couldn't hide the insult she was feeling. "Dora gets invited? Why does Dora get invited and I don't?"

"Because her power is waning and yours is on the

upswing. It hardly matters. What does matter is that she'll be there, and she'll be on our side when it goes down."

"What about the others?" Ofelia queried. "Will they be on our side?"

"Most of them will stay out of it. It's not as if Celeste has a lot of friends over there. Some might join in. We'll be fine, though."

Ofelia hoped that was true. "Get me at least one extra invitation if you can, please. We'll go from there."

"No problem. I'll text you as soon as I secure them."

"And I'll catch up Zach on the plan."

"Call me after lunch. We should have things fairly well planned out after that."

"Okay." Ofelia grabbed his wrist before he could get up. "Thank you for helping me."

"My dear, you're my family. Where else would I possibly be when you're in trouble?"

# 15
## FIFTEEN

Ofelia texted Sully to meet her in Jackson Square. She got an iced tea while she was waiting and watched the crowds. Even the vendor traffic was light right now because there were no tourists around. She couldn't remember the last time Jackson Square had been so quiet.

She felt Sully approaching before she saw him. When she turned, she was hit by how staggeringly beautiful he was. When she'd first met him, her initial thought was "could he be any hotter?" She didn't act on that impulse of course. They were both working the same case from different angles. He was so much more than his looks to her now, though. He was her best friend and confidant. Actually, he was her everything.

Sully must have sensed what she was feeling because he zeroed in on her when they locked gazes, making an immediate beeline for her. He caught her chin and graced her with a breathtaking kiss before he even uttered a single word in greeting.

Ofelia was breathless when they separated. "What was that for?" she gasped.

"You looked like you needed a kiss." He kept his grip on her face. "I know I needed one."

Ofelia let loose a rusty laugh. "Where is your father?"

"He's drinking his lunch at Krewe. I put Ben in charge of him. He seems better equipped to put up with his crap than me. I mean ... he doesn't even blink at the sexist nonsense that comes out of my father's mouth."

Ben was a man literally displaced in time. He'd been trapped on a steamboat by a malevolent entity for a hundred years, only being freed when the boat finally made it to New Orleans and Ofelia ended the entity. To Ofelia, it made sense that he could put up with Zeke's nonsense when they couldn't. He was a hundred years behind the progress that had been made, so Zeke's dated thinking was probably the sort of thing Ben was already accustomed to.

"He's used to women not having as many rights and building their whole lives around men," Ofelia mused. "I kind of get it."

"I'm over it." Sully gave her another kiss before releasing her. Then he reached for her iced tea. "I was happy to get your call. What's up?"

"I was thinking we would get lunch at Angelique's restaurant," Ofelia replied. Angelique Fleury was her best friend—well, other than Sully and Felix—and she just so happened to be a siren. "I want her to hear the update as well."

"Uh-oh." Sully had no trouble reading between the lines. "Are we about to go to war?"

"Are you going to be upset if I say yes?"

He looked torn. "I guess not." He exhaled heavily. "I was

hoping we would be able to get out of this one without a big fight. I guess not, huh?"

"Definitely not. We still have to pick our couple's costume for Halloween too if I'm going to rub it in to all those mean girls from high school. We can't forget that." Ofelia hadn't meant to say that part out loud, but once it was out, there was no hauling it back. "Or ... something that doesn't make me look like such an idiot," she muttered.

"Hold up." Sully raised his hand. "Is that what the costume mania is about? Are you trying to prove to the people you went to high school with that you're better than them?"

"Not *better* than them," Ofelia hedged. "I just want them to see how handsome you are, and if they get a load of my engagement ring and your muscles are accidentally put on display to enhance said engagement ring, what's the harm in that?"

Sully was caught between laughing and glaring. "Baby—"

"If you don't want to dress up in a couple's costume, you don't have to. I'm sorry I tried to force you." The quick way she averted her gaze told Sully that she didn't mean it.

"Oh, you're going to be a pain, aren't you?" he muttered. "I already told you that I'll wear a couple's costume ... within reason."

"I'm not going to be the socket to your plug," she warned.

He smirked. "And I'm not going to wear anything froufrou with tights. We both have our standards." He smoothed her hair. "I just didn't realize this was about sticking it to people you went to high school with."

"I didn't say I wanted to stick it to them. I just said I wanted them to see how hot you are."

"See, I want to be annoyed because that is vapid, but I like being considered hot. What does that say about me?"

"That you get me."

Sully took another sip of her iced tea before handing it back. "I do get you. We'll figure out a costume to make your former enemies cry. I promise. We need to deal with our current problem first."

"We do," Ofelia agreed, returning to reality. "I really don't want the mimes to ruin Halloween. That's our last hurrah before the break. We make good money that week."

"Forget the money. Nobody is going to question a mime running around during Halloween week. They'll think it's normal."

"There is that too." Ofelia finished off her iced tea and tossed the container in the nearest garbage can before grabbing Sully's hand. "Come on. I have a lot to fill you in on. I only want to tell the story once, though, so we need to find Angelique before I tell it."

"I'm going to hate this, aren't I?"

Ofelia considered it. "Probably, but I don't know what else to do."

"Then we'll do it."

*Just like that,* Ofelia mused. He didn't put up even a modicum of a fight. "You really do get me."

He cast her a wink and a smile. "I want to get you for the rest of our lives. That had better be decades and not hours, so let's get to it. I'm ready to kick the crap out of the mimes and get my father out of town."

"Ah, priorities. Let's do it."


**ANGELIQUE'S RESTAURANT ONLY OFFERED FANCY** menu items after five o'clock. Before then, it was all po' boys and potato salad. That was just what the doctor ordered, and Ofelia was enthusiastic when ordering.

"Someone has a big appetite," Angelique noted as the saucy siren stared down her friend. "Do I even want to know?"

"Probably not," Ofelia replied. "You don't get a choice in the matter, though. I think I'm going to need you."

"Uh-oh." Angelique stared at her for a beat, then nodded. "I'm due for a break in twenty minutes. I'll put your orders in, and when I come back with your food, we'll talk."

"Thank you."

By the time Angelique returned with their order, being sure to check on her other customers before sitting with them, there was a resigned tilt to her head. "Does this have something to do with the mimes that are running around?" she asked, making sure to keep her voice low.

"Well, at least we don't have to fill you in on the mimes," Sully said as he dug into his catfish po' boy. "That's something at least."

"What do you know?" Ofelia queried.

"I know that they've been seen hanging around the riverwalk," Angelique replied. "I know that most people ignored them the first few days because they assumed it was a gimmick."

"A gimmick?" Sully wiped the dressing from the corner of his mouth. "What sort of gimmick would involve mimes?"

Angelique shot him an "are you kidding me" look. "Dude, it's the French Quarter. Mimes would make a great way to announce the launch of a new voodoo shop ... or bar ... or even a random gift store. We expected them to carry around signs and lead people to whatever they were promoting. Only they weren't promoting anything."

"Huh." Sully hadn't considered it before. "That makes a little too much sense. It's hard when we live in a city where you can go days without triggering suspicion when dressed as a mime."

"Right?" Angelique bobbed her head. "People just ignored them at first. They might've said 'did you see the mime' but that's about it. That didn't last more than a few days, though."

"And why is that?" Sully queried.

"Because the mimes started stalking people. They would chase people to corners of the riverwalk, and even to hotels, and back them in corners. Then they would lean in real close, sniff them, and let them go."

Sully was officially appalled. "And nobody thought to call the police over that?"

"Not to beat a dead horse, but it's the French Quarter," Angelique reminded him. "I got sniffed by three separate guys on my way to work today. Although ... I do have a new perfume."

"This is unbelievable," Sully muttered.

"She's right," Ofelia said. She had dressing on her cheek from her po' boy but didn't care. "I get sniffed all the time. It's some weird French Quarter thing, I think."

Sully couldn't contain his grin when he reached over to wipe her cheek. "You are freaking adorable."

"Oh, how cute," Angelique drawled. "You're always cute, though. Let's go back to talking about the mimes."

"They were created by magic," Ofelia replied. "Celeste Cunningham to be exact. You're familiar with her, right?"

"We've met," Angelique said darkly. "Actually, to be

more precise, I've waited on her a time or two. She's a crappy tipper."

"Well, right now, she's conjuring mimes to track down and kill Zach's father," Ofelia explained.

Angelique's mouth fell open. "Are you kidding me right now?"

"Nope." Ofelia was solemn when shaking her head. "He set up a deal that was supposed to turn a corner of Audubon Park into a high-rise."

"Excuse my French, but your father is a jackass," Angelique barked at Sully.

He held up his hands in supplication. "You're preaching to the choir. I thought he was a jackass first."

"This isn't Zach's fault," Ofelia reminded Angelique. "As for Zeke, he's simply more worried about his bottom line than anything else. It doesn't matter, though. The environmentalists pulled the rug out from under him, and the project is dead."

"Well, that's good." Angelique was still sullen. "I can't believe that was almost a thing."

"Celeste lost twenty million in the deal, and now she's decided to pay back Zach's father with murderous mimes because of it," Ofelia explained.

"Well, no offense to Zach, but are we certain he doesn't deserve it?"

"I'm not," Sully replied. "I totally think he deserves it."

"It's not about deserving it," Ofelia argued. "It's about keeping the Quarter safe. Those three bodies that were found on Bourbon Street yesterday were innocents. The mimes essentially fed on them for sport."

"That is just so gross." Angelique leaned back in her chair. "Is there a way we can kill the mimes and still make Zach's father pay?"

"We can't worry about punishing Zeke," Ofelia insisted. "That can't be our priority. We have to hope that karma will get him ... in the form of Zach's mother or something. We have to focus on Celeste and the mimes."

"How are we sure that Celeste is responsible for this?" Angelique queried. "It's not that I'm questioning you or anything—because I'm not—but how can we be sure that it's her?"

"Because I went to visit her at her office this morning, and she admitted it," Ofelia replied. "I'm not talking about admitting it without admitting it or anything either. She flat out said it was her and didn't seem ashamed in the least."

"Oh, well, that's lovely." Angelique made a face. "I've never liked her, and it's not just because she's the world's worst tipper. She walks around as if she's the most important person in the Quarter and everybody else should bow down because she deigns to spend time in our neighborhood."

"She's never been pleasant," Ofelia agreed. "I didn't realize she was as much of a concern as she is, though ... until now. We have no choice but to deal with her."

"And how do we do that?"

"We're going to the Celestial Cabaret party tonight and taking her—and likely her mimes—out."

Whatever Sully and Angelique were expecting, that wasn't it. Their eyes went wide in tandem as their mouths fell open. Sully was the first to recover. "What now?" he said finally.

"I stopped to see Pascal on my way back from talking to Dora," Ofelia explained. "He said that Celeste is on the planning committee for the party, and attendance is mandatory. He's going to get us a few invitations."

"To the Celestial Cabaret party?" Sully made an exaggerated face. "Fe, no offense, but that is not a place where we're going to fit in."

Now it was Ofelia's turn to make a face. "Whenever someone says, 'No offense' they're about to offend you," she noted. "Why aren't those our people?"

Sully refused to be drawn into a fight. "You know why. They're hoity-toity, and we're not. That's not our crowd. Don't give me grief for saying the obvious."

"I'm not giving you grief," Ofelia assured him. "I just think it's our best shot. She won't be expecting us there. By tomorrow, she'll have prepared herself for whatever trap we try to set. If we do it tonight, we'll be assured of a paranormal audience."

"Doesn't that worry you?" Angelique queried. "Because it worries me. We don't know who her friends are."

"Pascal doesn't seem to think she has a lot of friends."

"How familiar is Pascal with her, though?" Sully challenged.

"He goes to the Cabaret every year. He's the one who told me about the party, and that she was on the planning committee. He thinks it's our best shot."

"Is it going to be our best shot if she has more friends than he realizes, and they all move on us?" Sully challenged.

"Probably not." Ofelia refused to explode because a fight wouldn't benefit any of them right now. "If you have a better idea, I'm open to entertaining it." She hoped she sounded rational because she was toeing a fine line.

"Um ... I say we do nothing and let my father clean up his own mess."

"And I might be persuaded to agree with you—although probably not—if it weren't for one thing."

Sully was already ahead of her. "You mean the dead bodies the mimes are dropping."

"Celeste said that the mimes are feeding," Ofelia replied. "We can't just allow that to keep happening. You can't possibly think that's allowable."

"No, I don't." Sully wiped the corners of his mouth with his napkin and threw it on his plate. "I'm just frustrated because I feel my father should be dealing with this mess. It shouldn't fall on us."

"I don't disagree. We're stuck with it though."

Sully made a grumbling sound deep in his throat.

Angelique, sensing trouble, prodded the conversation along. "How are we going to play this? I mean ... are you sure you can beat her?"

"I'm on the fence on that one," Ofelia admitted. "Pascal is certain I can beat her, though. Plus, well, apparently Dora will be there."

"And we know she'll take your side because she hates Celeste," Angelique surmised.

"Well, since Celeste tried to kill her, that goes without saying," Ofelia replied. "She'll definitely be on our side, though. She might not actively try to kill Celeste with us, but if she senses we're losing, she'll help. I know she will."

"Crap." Sully shook his head. "We're really doing this, aren't we?"

"I don't see where we have a choice," Ofelia replied. "We have to go after her when she's not expecting us. Come tomorrow, she'll be expecting us. She won't be expecting us at the Celestial Cabaret tonight, though."

"No, she definitely won't." Sully started bobbing his head. "Fine. We'll do this. How is it going to work?"

"I figured we would just go, back her into a corner, and

either bind her powers or kill her and the mimes that she calls in to protect her."

"Oh, is that what you thought?" Sully barked out a hollow laugh. "Fe, that is unbelievable. We can't just go in there and wing it."

"Why not? That's what we usually do."

"I know but..." He trailed off, looking to Angelique for support. "Tell her."

"What do you need from me?" Angelique asked instead.

"I might need a tsunami," Ofelia replied. "You know, a distraction of some sort."

"I can handle that," Angelique assured her. "We'll take Ben, too. He doesn't have a lot of magic at his disposal, but I'm betting he can take on a mime or two. When we're both dressed up, people will assume we're a couple and won't think twice about questioning why we're there." She looked so thrilled at the prospect, Ofelia was taken aback.

"Um ... are you and Ben dating now?" she asked.

Angelique's smile disappeared in an instant. "No. Why would you think that?"

"Because you seem excited about going on a date with him."

"That's not a date."

"Um ... I think it is."

"No. It's just a magical outing. We go on magical outings all the time. We don't consider them dates."

She was a bit too defensive for Ofelia's comfort level. "You know it's okay to date him, right?" Ofelia prodded. "He's a free man. His last girlfriend died a hundred years ago."

"Not really. She was stuck in a time loop with him. Her soul was trapped at least. He only said his goodbyes a few months ago."

Ofelia remained suspicious but opted not to push Angelique too hard. "Well, whatever you're calling it, I think including Ben is a good idea. We're going to need to get him a suit, though."

"I'll handle that." Angelique's smile was back. "You guys just worry about how you're going to dress."

"Ah, another costume," Sully lamented. "I can't wait."

Ofelia pinned him with a dark look. "If you don't want to go, it's not necessary." She decided playing hardball was the only way to get him to stop complaining. "In fact, I think the best thing to do is for me to handle it myself. You can do ... whatever it is you want to do. I know, why don't you go whine with your dad, huh? That should help things."

With that, she dug in her purse for some cash and handed it to Angelique to cover their bill. "I'll text you with the details," she promised before turning to leave.

"Ofelia, don't be like that," Sully called to her back. He was flummoxed at her reaction. "I was just kidding."

She didn't respond. Instead, she kept going. He was on her last nerve, and she had no idea what to do about it.

# 16

## SIXTEEN

Sully didn't immediately chase Ofelia. Instead, he remained in his seat. He could feel Angelique's gaze on him, but he didn't know how to explain what had just happened, so he sat in silence like a big loser instead.

"You guys don't normally fight," she said after a few seconds.

"We don't," he agreed. "We're not fighting now either."

"That kind of looked like a fight to me," she hedged.

"Well, it wasn't." Sully drummed his fingers on top of the table. "Just how long after an exchange of words should I wait before I get up and chase her? I don't want to come across as weak."

Angelique pressed her lips together to keep from laughing. "An exchange of words?"

"That's what it was."

"But not a fight."

"We don't fight." Sully was insistent. "Not really at least. We're just facing a tense time."

"Because of your father?"

"And her father ... and her mother. If I'm being honest, my mother doesn't help either. She's not often here, though."

Angelique chuckled. "There's no reason to get worked up, you know. It's going to be okay. She won't stay mad."

"I know. It's just ... I feel as if she deserves more than this. She has to go in and fight my father's enemy because otherwise innocent people are going to die. Why does it always fall on her?"

"Because she's the strongest person I know," Angelique replied simply. "She fights for all the people who don't have the strength to fight for themselves. She was always going to go after Celeste. Even if it wasn't your father involved, she wouldn't have allowed the mimes to keep killing people. You realize that, right?"

He swallowed hard and nodded.

"You're trying to save her from your father, and that's not how it works," Angelique continued. "She's going to finish this. You can't stop her. So, instead of being a Debbie Downer when it comes to her idea, just support her and stop being a douche."

He made a face. "I'm not trying to be a douche."

"Of course you're not." Angelique sounded utterly reasonable. "You're trying to protect her and she's trying to protect you and things are a mess because of outside forces. It is what it is."

"My father always makes things worse," Sully complained. "I don't want him to make things worse for her."

"I don't think you get a say in the matter," Angelique replied. "You guys have no choice but to face this stuff together. You can't save each other from the bad stuff. You have to enjoy the good stuff and muddle through the rest."

"I know." He tapped his fingers as he regarded her. "Do you like Ben?" he asked out of nowhere, changing the subject.

"And on that note." Angelique stood and pinned him with a "back off" look. "Tell Ofelia I'll text her when I have outfits picked out. I'll handle telling Ben, too, and not because it's a date. It's because you guys have your hands full."

Sully's lips quirked. "How long do you expect us to fall for that?"

"As long as is necessary."

"If you say so." He stood and threw an extra twenty on the table. "Thanks for the therapy session. Just out of curiosity, what makes you think I'm going to find her? Why wouldn't I just let her do what she wants to do and go to the party alone?"

"Because that's not who either of you are."

"Good point." He leaned in and gave Angelique a half-hearted hug. "I hate it when we fight."

"So, go make up. You know where she's heading."

"She's going to see Oscar."

Angelique nodded. "I knew that. How did you know it, though?"

"Because when she feels out of control, she needs to see her dad and be reminded that there are worse things than having a bad day."

"That's pretty much true. Just go to her and tell her you're a tool and you're sorry."

"How come I'm always the one who has to apologize?"

"Do you think you were in the right here?"

"I'm not talking about today. I'm talking about all the other times."

"How about you just focus on today for now, and we'll deal with the other times later, huh?"

On a sigh, Sully nodded. "I guess that will have to work."

"I think it's the best option for both of you," Angelique agreed. "I'll be in touch after my shift."

"We'll be waiting for you."


**OSCAR WAS WORKING ON A PUZZLE WHEN OFELIA** walked into his room. He only looked up when she sat with him and wordlessly started fitting pieces. He studied her a moment, debating, and then went back to work.

They toiled like that for a good ten minutes before either of them spoke.

"Do you want to talk about it?" he asked.

"I don't know. I'm just sick of people today."

"Any people in particular?"

"Zach."

"That won't last."

He sounded so sure of himself, Ofelia let her insides relax a little bit. "His father is a butthead too."

"I've met his father. He's definitely a butthead."

"There are murderous mimes on the loose because of his father," Ofelia explained. "I have to get into a witch fight to make sure they stop killing people, and the whole thing makes me mad."

Oscar stilled. "Are you going to be in danger?"

Ofelia wasn't certain how to respond to the question. "I'll be fine," she said finally. "You don't have to worry about me."

"You're my daughter. That goes with the territory."

Ofelia nodded. That made sense. Well, except for one

little thing. "Zach's father never puts him first, and I'm mad. I'm mad on Zach's behalf. I'm mad because Zach always puts me first, and I can't help but wonder where he learned to do that if neither of his parents acted as proper role models. I'm just mad, mad, mad."

Oscar was silent for so long that Ofelia figured he'd tuned out. When she looked over, though, she found him grinning.

"It's not funny." Ofelia sank lower in the chair and folded her arms across her chest. "I hate his dad. He's a jerk."

"There, there." Oscar patted Ofelia's shoulder but didn't say anything else.

"That's it? No pep talk?"

"Well, I could go with my gut and tell you to break up with him," Oscar started.

Ofelia made a disgruntled sound deep in her throat.

"Or I could do the smart thing and let it go," he continued. "It's not as if you guys are going to fight forever or anything. You'll make up within the hour if I have to lay odds on it."

"I just told you I'm mad," Ofelia reminded him.

"You're not mad at him. You're mad at the situation." The sound of footsteps had Oscar turning his attention to the door, to where Sully stood. "I told you."

Ofelia followed his gaze and scowled when she found her fiancé watching the scene. "I'm not in the mood," she warned him.

"I know." Sully plopped down on Oscar's bed without invitation and pulled out his phone. "I'm going to sort through couple's costume ideas while you sulk. Tell me when you're ready for the apology."

"I'm not apologizing."

"I was talking about me."

"Oh." Ofelia moved her neck back and forth. "I'm not ready for that either," she said finally.

"I know." Sully focused on his phone screen. "How about Adam and Eve?"

"Does that involve us being naked except for fig leaves?" Ofelia queried.

"Yes."

"Absolutely not. We'll get mistaken for strippers."

He couldn't disagree. "Care Bears are out," he muttered to himself.

"Why are they out?" Ofelia challenged. She'd decided to be difficult just to be difficult. "I might want to be a Care Bear."

"I thought the whole point was for your former classmates to see how hot I am?" Sully challenged. "They can't do that if I'm in Care Bear mode."

"Oh, is that why you're doing it?" Oscar demanded. "I was having trouble keeping up. Of course you're doing it for those idiots you went to high school with. You're still upset about losing that other costume contest."

Ofelia made a sniffing noise. "I am not upset."

"She was depressed for two weeks," Oscar volunteered to Sully. "I brought ice cream home to her every single day, and it did very little good. Ice cream was always the trick to getting her out of a funk."

"I'm prepared to dress up," Sully assured him. "I simply have my limits." He made a popping noise with his lips. "Cave people are out. As much as I like the outfit for you, I am not running around with a mullet wig and a loin cloth. The spear is a nice touch, though."

He continued scrolling. "There's a cops and robbers

one. It would be fun for us because I would be the robber and you would be wearing a sexy cop uniform."

The look Ofelia shot him was withering.

"You said no food. Oh, the Frankenstein and his bride one is cool. That's a lot of green paint, though." Sully's eyes moved toward her. "It might be kind of hot after the party. I mean ... the green paint might be intriguing."

"I don't want to be covered in green paint," Ofelia shot back. "I want to look sexy."

"You would be sexy in a burlap sack."

"Hey!" Oscar shot him a dirty look. "Don't say stuff like that to my daughter."

"Sorry." Sully wasn't really sorry. "What about this?" He held up the photo for Ofelia to see. "I could be a gangster and you could be a flapper. The costume for me won't elicit too many snickers from my co-workers and you would fill out that dress in all the right places."

"Hey!" Oscar stomped his foot. "What did I say?"

Sully ignored him. All he cared about was Ofelia at this point.

"I actually don't hate that idea," Ofelia hedged. "We can put that in the maybe column."

"Oh, we finally have a maybe." Sully was thrilled. "It only took us the better part of a week."

Ofelia went back to helping her father with the puzzle. "We have to go after Celeste, Zach," she said in a low voice when he'd been quiet for a full minute. "We can't do nothing. I know you're angry with your father—and you have every right to be—but we have to do something before more innocent people die."

"I know." There was no accusation in his tone. "I got angry because this was falling on you even though it wasn't your mess, and I shouldn't have snapped the way I did."

"I think I snapped a little too," she admitted. "I didn't mean to. It's just ... your dad sucks."

Sully burst out laughing. "It's funny that you seem to think that's news to me."

"I always assumed I was going to like him better than your mother for some reason," Ofelia admitted. "When I think back on it, I realize you were mostly evasive when I asked about your father. I didn't press enough, though, and that makes me feel guilty for an entirely different reason."

"And what reason is that?"

"I was so caught up in my stuff that I didn't ask about your stuff," Ofelia replied. "You always go out of your way for me, and yet I didn't even bother to ask the obvious question for you."

"No." Sully shook his head before shifting to the side of the bed and patting it. "Come here, Fe."

"Don't do it in my bed," Oscar warned when Ofelia vacated her chair and rolled in next to Sully. She immediately buried her face in his chest.

"I'm starting to get the feeling that you believe you're a bad girlfriend," Sully said as he rubbed his hands up and down her back. "That couldn't be further from the truth."

"It's worse than that," Ofelia argued. "I'm a bad fiancée. We're going to get married in the foreseeable future, and I've let you down."

"No, you haven't." Sully was stern when he lifted his head. "You haven't let me down at all. If anything, I've let you down because ... well, because I didn't want to talk about him. I made it easy to talk about different things for a reason."

"And why is that?" Ofelia asked.

"Yeah, *why* is that?" Oscar echoed. He'd completely lost

interest in his puzzle and was now focused on his daughter and future son-in-law.

"Because your family is completely up in each other's business, to the point where you're all codependent," Sully replied.

"That is not a compliment."

He laughed. "But it is. You guys all love each other. Even your mother loves you and Felix. Heck, she still loves Oscar in her own way."

"She's got a funny way of showing it," Oscar shot back.

"She does," Ofelia agreed.

"It doesn't matter how she shows it. She feels it. My parents are ... *removed* ... from my life."

Ofelia immediately started shaking her head. "Your mother loves you. Tell me you don't think otherwise."

"My mother does love me," he agreed. "She loves me a great deal. She just ... withholds that love when I don't do what she wants. When she's disinterested in what I'm doing, she becomes disinterested in me. She'll come back around when we start planning the wedding in earnest, but if it's not her idea, she doesn't like it."

Ofelia considered it for several seconds, then sighed. He wasn't wrong. "And your father?"

"He's not a bad guy when you compare him to fathers who actively try to hurt their kids," Sully replied. "He's just ... oblivious. He would never purposely try to hurt me or my mother or anybody else in my family for that matter. He just can't see beyond himself."

"That doesn't make him a good guy," Ofelia pointed out.

"It doesn't, but there are worse guys out there."

Ofelia lifted her finger to trace his cheek. "How did you get to be the best guy when you have him as a father?"

"I knew at a young age that I wanted to be different from him," Sully replied. "I didn't want to be tied up in pack politics. I didn't want to be fixated on business above all else. I just wanted to be a good man who helped people."

"Well, you've accomplished that."

Sully pulled her tight against him and rested his cheek on her forehead. When he shifted slightly, he found Oscar watching them with unreadable eyes. "We should probably stop taking over your room, huh?" he said after a beat.

Oscar immediately started shaking his head. "It's okay. You can stay. I'm fine with it." He went back to his puzzle. "It makes me feel like I'm at home again. You guys were mushy messes back then, too."

Sully smirked. "We were mushy messes. I promise we'll stay mushy messes just for you."

"Ha, ha." Oscar's eyes were clearer than Sully could ever remember them, and he understood now why Ofelia was so hopeful. In a moment like this, when Oscar was better than he'd likely ever been, anything seemed possible.

Unfortunately, nothing remained the same forever.

"Did Ofelia mention the family counseling to you?" Oscar queried.

"She did," Sully confirmed.

"You should be there."

Sully was suddenly choked up. "Because I'm part of the family?"

"Oh, don't get schmaltzy," Oscar warned. "I want you to be there for my kids. You keep it together better than the three of us do combined sometimes. That's all I'm saying. Don't go thinking I'm falling in love with you or anything."

Sully pressed his lips together in an effort to keep from laughing. "I'll do my best," he said when he was reasonably assured he could speak without laughing.

"Any ideas on couple's costumes while you're doling out wisdom?"

"Um ... yeah." Oscar shot him a "well, duh" look. "You should be Morticia and Gomez. Sure, you'll have to make your hair look stupid, but otherwise it's just a suit. Ofelia will get to wear a pretty dress, and her hair already fits the costume. It will be easy and perfect."

Sully opened his mouth to laugh off the suggestion, and then tilted his head as he truly considered it. "Huh," he said finally.

"I would look really good in a Morticia dress," Ofelia mused.

"You would look amazing in a Morticia dress," Sully agreed.

"And nobody would make fun of you for dressing up like Gomez," she added.

"Mostly nobody. At least one or two of them would give me grief. Nothing too terrible, though."

"Do you think we can pull it off?"

Sully shifted so he was looking directly into her eyes. "I think we can pull anything off ... including what we're going to have to deal with tonight. If I haven't said it already—and I've honestly lost count of what we've talked about—I'm all in on the plan. I know we have to take Celeste out."

"And dress up for the Celestial Cabaret?"

Sully made a face. "And dress up for the Celestial Cabaret," he acknowledged. "I still maintain those aren't our people, though."

"They probably aren't," Ofelia agreed. "It doesn't matter, though. Our people are going to die on the street if we don't do something. I can't allow more blood on my conscience. We have to end it tonight."

"We will." Sully was grim. "For better or worse, we're going to have to take out Celeste and the mimes."

"Yeah. Now we just have to figure out how to do it."

"It would be nice to go in there with a plan."

"Yeah. Any ideas?"

"No, but we have a few hours. Let's start figuring it out."

# 17
## SEVENTEEN

Zeke was at the bar when Ofelia and Sully let themselves into Krewe. The dark look Ofelia shot him was enough to have Sully prodding her toward the stairs.

"I'll take care of him," Sully promised. "Why don't you head up and take a long bath, huh? We have hours before the party, and I think you need to unwind."

Ofelia's eyes narrowed as she debated. Ultimately, she nodded. "He can't go." She pointed at Zeke for emphasis. "He'll make things worse, and we don't need the distraction."

"He's not going," Sully promised. "I am, however, calling the paranormal unit for backup."

The admission threw Ofelia. "You are?" She didn't know how to feel about it. On one hand, she didn't know what they could do to help. On the other, knowing there was a layer of protection between the mimes and the rest of the city was a relief.

"I am," he agreed. "We need them there just in case.

People will be at risk from the mimes if this doesn't go our way."

Ofelia nodded in understanding. There was little the paranormal unit could do about Celeste if it came to a fight. They could, however, handle the mimes. "Okay." She forced a smile she didn't feel. "I'm going to go up and take that bath. I need to pick out a dress, too."

"Pick something I'm going to enjoy taking off of you later," he suggested.

"Oh, I was going to pick something that I'm not going to cry about if it gets ruined."

"That works too." Sully watched her go, his stomach constricting. She obviously had a lot on her mind, and since she was the one who would be fighting Celeste, almost all of the pressure was on her. He didn't like it.

To combat his negative feelings, he planted himself on the stool next to Zeke and signaled Ben for a beer.

"Are you sure you don't want anything stronger?" Ben queried as Sully thanked him for the beer. "Angelique called. I know we're ... heading out on a special mission ... this evening."

"I don't want to blunt my edges too much," Sully replied. "We'll hit the hard stuff when we're done."

Ben nodded in understanding. "I'll let you guys get to it then."

Sully sipped his beer and waited for Ben to wander away. It was too early in the day for the bar to be busy, but there were several locals hanging out. Thankfully, they were all at the end of the bar.

"Am I missing something?" Zeke queried when Sully hadn't spoken in several minutes.

"Oh, so many things," Sully drawled. His annoyance was obvious when he focused on his father and took another sip. "I have some things I want to say to you," he volunteered after a few seconds. "For once, I want you to listen to what I have to say and not be you."

"I have no idea what that means," Zeke said blankly.

"I'm sure you don't. That doesn't change the fact that I have some things I want to say to you." Sully took another drink, building up his liquid courage. "You're a crappy father," he blurted out of nowhere, catching Zeke off guard. "Just ... the absolute worst. I know that Grandpa Sully was a crappy father to you, and you were just emulating what you'd learned, but you suck. You suck the big one."

Rather than roll his eyes and make a big show of denying it, Zeke nodded. "I am the worst father known to man," he agreed. "If it's any consolation, I didn't know going in that I was going to be such a terrible father. I thought I was going to be a good father. I assumed I was going to be better than my father. I was wrong."

Sully couldn't decide how to proceed. He'd assumed his father would deny the charge, which would allow him to build to a crescendo when explaining exactly why his father sucked. That didn't appear to be happening, though.

"If you know you're a crappy father, why don't you try to change?" Sully snapped finally. "Why not try to become a better father?"

"Because I think it's best when people acknowledge their limitations. I am limited as a father. I'm limited as a husband, too. Your mother accepts me for who I am and makes allowances for my behavior, but that just enables me."

Sully's mouth dropped open. "Why are you using the word 'enables' suddenly? How do you even know that word?"

"My therapist explained it to me."

"You're in therapy?" Sully was incredulous. "What in the hell?"

Zeke chuckled. "Just because I acknowledge that I'm terrible, that doesn't mean I don't want to get better. I do. I know I'm not the father you deserve. I'm working on it."

"You're working on it," Sully drawled, dumbfounded. He had no idea how he was supposed to respond. This conversation wasn't going how he'd anticipated.

"I am definitely working on it," Zeke agreed. "Your mother and I are even in couple's counseling. Or, well, we were. Then she found out a witch was trying to kill me, and she said not to come back until I had it under control and was serious about making things right with my family."

"And you listened to her?" Sully had trouble wrapping his head around it. "Since when do you listen to Mom?"

"Your mother is a very intelligent woman."

"I know my mother is a very intelligent woman. I just didn't know you knew it."

Zeke's eye roll was pronounced. "I know you can't see it because you're used to me running my mouth and saying one thing and not following through, but I really do love your mother."

"Actually, I do know that," Sully acknowledged. "That's the one thing I've never doubted where you're concerned."

"I don't cheat on her. I never have."

Sully hesitated.

"I get that you have your doubts because I like to flirt, but that's a business thing," Zeke insisted. "I love your mother. I also acknowledge she deserves better. I would like to give her that 'better' going forward. I just ... don't know how."

Sully was utterly flabbergasted. "Well, for starters, you could stop flirting with random women," he suggested.

"That's knee-jerk, but I will work on it."

"Including my fiancée."

Now Zeke smirked. "The girl is special."

"I know she's special. That's why I'm going to marry her."

"You know I can't ignore a woman who is beautiful, strong, and has a mouth like that. She's like a younger version of your mother. I can't help myself."

Sully's first instinct was to deny it. There was no way Ofelia was like his mother. Yet, when he broke it down, he realized his father was right. Ofelia was very much like his mother ... and wasn't that a terrifying thought? "Oh, no way." Sully downed the rest of his beer and motioned for Ben to get him another.

"Are you freaking out?" Zeke queried.

"You have no idea."

Zeke chuckled. He was beyond amused. "Having a strong woman isn't a bad thing. In fact, it's a nice thing overall. Whenever a business associate claims he wants a submissive partner, I don't get it. How boring would that be? If you don't have a woman who challenges you, what's the point?"

"I have no idea," Sully admitted. "I just ... crap. I'm going to have nightmares now."

Zeke laughed again as Ben delivered Sully's beer, giving him a hefty shoulder clap. He was serious when he stopped laughing. "Tell me what the plan is."

Sully filled him in. There was no sense avoiding the subject. When he was finished, Zeke was laser focused on the path forward.

"Do we really think this is going to work?" Zeke queried.

"Ofelia does. Pascal does."

"What's with her and the vampire?" Zeke queried. "I

have questions, but I'm afraid to ask them ... for obvious reasons. Pascal has always been a bit of an enigma. I'm not sure if he hates me, or if he just pretends to hate me."

"Oh, he hates you," Sully assured his father. "With a fiery passion. He would never do anything to you because you're my father, though."

"And he loves you," Zeke surmised.

"No, he tolerates me. He might like me on random days. He loves Ofelia, though, and she loves me. That means he would die to protect me because it's what Ofelia needs."

Zeke nodded in understanding. "I get it."

Did he? On a different day, Sully would've said that wasn't possible. Thanks to Zeke's new self-awareness kick, he wasn't as certain about that today. "Pascal helped Oscar when Ofelia was young. I think they were friends, although I've started to wonder if Pascal was always in love with Ofelia—not in a gross way or anything—and he only hung around to make sure she was safe. Oscar's mental illness put Ofelia in danger more than once."

"And yet she still loves her father."

"So very much," Sully agreed. "When Katrina hit, Pascal carried Ofelia through a flooding French Quarter to get her and Oscar to safety. They've been bonded ever since. He would die for her."

"And that doesn't bother you? I mean ... you don't find it creepy? His attachment to her could mean bad things for you."

"It bothered me at first, but his attachment to her isn't romantic. He fancies himself her second father, and their relationship is nothing to worry about."

"You're a better man than me."

"I am," Sully readily agreed. "You still have a chance to become a better man, though. Don't blow it."

Zeke's eyes flashed with annoyance. "I said I was working on it."

"Then keep at it." Sully rolled his neck. "As for Pascal, he'll be there tonight. I'm glad for it. There's an off chance he could kill Celeste if she's distracted, and he can move in behind her. All he needs is to get his hands on her."

Realization dawned on Zeke. "You don't want Ofelia to be the one who has to kill her."

"I would prefer that she not be the one, but I'm realistic."

"It's not as if Celeste is a good person. She wouldn't be killing some innocent."

"No, but this shouldn't be her fight. It should be my fight. You're my father. I can't take out the witch, though, which means Ofelia is on deck."

"She's more powerful than you." Zeke said it with equal parts awe and worry. "Magically at least, she's more powerful than you."

"She's the most powerful person I know," Sully agreed. "That's another reason I was drawn to her the way I was."

"It's freaky. I don't think I could be with a woman who is more powerful than me."

"You already are. You just don't realize it."

Zeke opened his mouth to argue but seemed to think better of it. "What do you want me to do tonight?"

"Nothing."

Zeke was certain he'd heard his son wrong. "Nothing? This is my fight. Shouldn't I be involved?"

"Celeste wants you dead. We can't afford for the two of you to be in the same room together because she might kill others to get to you. It's best that you're not part of this particular fight. You should stay here."

"But..." Zeke worked his jaw, up and down. Ultimately,

he nodded. "Okay. I guess I don't have a choice in the matter."

"You don't," Sully agreed. "We're going in with some friends. Pascal and Dora will be there. Ofelia hopes to back Celeste in a corner, kill the mimes, and bind Celeste. When that doesn't work—and even she knows it won't—then she'll kill her. She won't have a choice."

"And that's it? Just like that it will be over?"

"Just like that," Sully confirmed.

Zeke finished off his drink. "It almost seems too easy," he admitted after several seconds.

"Maybe to you, but it seems like a big risk for the woman I love. If something happens to her, I'll never get over it. You realize that, right?"

"Of course I do. You love her, just like I love your mother."

"I'll die for her if it comes to it."

Zeke swallowed hard. "I know. You're a true hero."

"No, I'm a man who can't live without the woman he loves. Just ... stay here and stay out of trouble. Do you think you can manage that?"

"Of course. I'm excellent at staying out of trouble."

"Right. I guess there's a first time for everything."


**ON A DIFFERENT NIGHT, OFELIA MIGHT HAVE** gotten excited about slipping into a pretty dress—one that showed off her angular curves—and heading out with Sully on her arm. Given what they were facing tonight, however, she felt otherwise.

"What are you thinking?" Sully asked as they waited in line to get inside the huge Garden District mansion that would be hosting the Celestial Cabaret. "Do you want to turn back?"

Ofelia shook her head. "No. I'm a little nervous—especially because I'm wearing heels, and I can't run in them—but I still maintain this is the only thing we can do at this point."

Because he didn't disagree, Sully nodded. He had her hand tucked through his arm as they waited, and he patted her fingers more than once. Angelique and Ben were behind them, several couples separating them. It had been agreed that they wouldn't draw attention to the fact that they were entering as a foursome.

"I hope they at least have good food," Ofelia said out of nowhere. "If I'm going to start killing mimes, I want stuffed mushrooms for my effort."

Sully cast her a sidelong look. "I'll get you stuffed mushrooms regardless. You have my word."

Ofelia grinned at him. "See. Now there's something to look forward to. Can we eat them in bed?"

"Baby, I'm going to keep you in bed for the entire weekend as soon as this is done," he promised her in a flirty voice.

She wiggled her hips to express her excitement, then focused on the woman checking the invitations by the door. "Honor Carloff," she said in a low voice.

Sully followed her gaze. "You know her?"

"She's a witch."

"One of Celeste's?"

Ofelia hesitated, then lifted one shoulder. "I don't know her well. I've always thought of her as a solitary practitioner. Your father said that Celeste always had two witches at her side, though. Honor could be the brunette he mentioned."

Sully nodded. His gaze had latched on to another figure on the other side of the door. "And Jane Carmichael would be the blonde." He wasn't happy when he saw her. "She makes love potions and sells them to the highest bidder. She's caused more than one murder-suicide because of them. We just can't prove it."

Ofelia followed his gaze. "Well, if you're lucky, that also might not be an issue after tonight."

"Don't eat anything here," Sully said. "When they see us, they're going to know ... and I wouldn't put it past Jane to try to dose us with one of her potions."

Ofelia had already come to that conclusion herself. "We'll find stuffed mushrooms on the way home."

"We will," Sully promised. "We'll pick up a whole buffet of food and eat it in bed."

Ofelia held her breath when Honor checked their invitation. She could feel the witch's speculative gaze roam over her and Sully, but she held it together and didn't say anything. Instead, she merely smiled ... and waited.

"Ofelia Archer," Honor said after a beat. "I didn't know you were invited."

"I guess I'm coming up in the world," Ofelia replied in easy fashion.

"Uh-huh." Honor stared at the invitation for a beat longer and then handed it back. "Have a great time."

"That's the plan." Ofelia kept her smile in place as Sully led her past Jane. She felt like a frog that was about to be dissected under a magnifying glass, but she forced herself not to react outwardly.

"Don't drink anything either," Sully said as they made their way into the ballroom. He clearly wasn't happy at the amount of people hanging around. "I had no idea there were so many paranormals in New Orleans," he complained when he managed to take in the full scope of the room. "Wow."

Ofelia leaned in close as his arm moved around her waist. He was determined to keep her anchored to his side, and she was fine with that ... for now. When it was time to fight, she wanted him as far away from the action as possible.

That was an issue for later, though.

"What do you think?" Angelique asked as she arrived behind them.

Ofelia glanced over her shoulder and let loose a low whistle when she saw how low cut Angelique's dress was. "Hello, boobs," she said automatically without thinking.

Sully practically choked. "Um ... that is a weird thing to say."

"Sorry." Ofelia shook her head. "She's just got a lot of boobs going on there."

"They'll make for a nice distraction," Angelique replied.

"I'll say," Ben agreed. His gaze couldn't be torn away from Angelique's dress, which looked as if it were being held in place by duct tape. "What were we talking about again?" he asked as he forced his gaze up from Angelique's dress and focused on Ofelia. "Do we have a plan yet?"

"Not yet," Ofelia replied. "Once I see Celeste, I think the plan will be to separate from the group, try to talk to her, and when that fails, I'll wing it."

"And we're just here to deal with the mimes?" Angelique queried.

"I'm pretty sure, as soon as Celeste realizes I'm here, that the mimes will be coming out to play," Ofelia confirmed. "There's always a chance that she'll keep them at bay, but I'm not holding my breath." She glanced at Sully, who had raised his nose and was clearly scenting the air.

"Anything?" she asked, unsure what he could possibly be looking for.

"Can you figure out where Celeste is by her scent?" Ben asked. He looked impressed. "That would be helpful."

"I have no idea what Celeste smells like," Sully replied. He was grim. "I do know what my father smells like, however."

Ofelia's nose wrinkled. "Why would that matter unless...?" She trailed off. Her stomach constricted when she realized what he hadn't said. "Crap."

Sully nodded. "Despite the fact that I told him we would be handling this, my father clearly decided to serve as a distraction. He's here ... somewhere."

Ofelia looked around at the packed soirée. "Well, we'd better find him." She was resigned. "I guarantee, wherever he is, Celeste won't be far behind."

"And she won't hold back," Sully added. "This is definitely going down tonight."

# 18

## EIGHTEEN

They separated into couples, but only because Sully immediately shot down Ofelia's suggestion that they might be better off if they split the room into four grids and started looking as individuals. He reminded her that he was the only one who could scent his father, and since they were convinced Celeste would be with him when they found him, it only made sense that they should stick together.

Ofelia felt otherwise—she didn't want Sully to serve as collateral damage when the magic started flying—but she didn't put up a fight. Instead, she let Sully lead the way ... until he led her right out of the ballroom.

"Wait." Ofelia grasped at his arm when he moved to leave through a closed door. "I don't think we're supposed to leave this area."

Sully shot her an exaggerated look. "I love that you're such a good girl you want to follow the rules at a party where my father might be killed, but I'm a police officer. If someone gives us crap, I'll flash my badge and call for the reinforcements to join us."

Even though Ofelia knew that the paranormal division had sent an entire battalion of soldiers to collapse on the house—they were right now amassing in two separate trucks one street over—she was still nervous. "Maybe you should stay here, and I'll head out to search," she suggested.

"What did I say?" Sully's agitation came out to play. "We're not separating."

"I know but..." Ofelia was at a loss. Finally, she said the only thing she could say ... even though she knew Sully wouldn't want to hear it. "Celeste will use your presence to torture your father. I think you should stay here."

"No. I'm going with you."

"I don't want you getting tortured."

"Then you'd better smite her quick." Sully grabbed Ofelia's shoulders and pressed a loud kiss against her forehead. "Baby, we're in this together," he said in a low voice. "For better or worse, we're a team. You can't protect me on this one."

Ofelia wanted to argue—she was desperate to keep Sully out of the line of fire—but she recognized that she would be furious if their roles were reversed, and he tried to keep her out of the mix. Ultimately, she nodded. "If I tell you to do something, you need to do it," she whispered.

"Okay." He flashed a smile. "You're the expert on this one. I'll do what you say."

That was far too easy, Ofelia mused. He was either lying or she'd missed something.

"I'm going to be the expert in the bedroom tonight when this is over," he added. "Then you have to do what I say."

"And there it is," she muttered. "Fine. We're taking

stuffed mushrooms, cheesecake, and chicken wings home to eat in bed, though."

"That's quite the refined palette you've got there," he drawled. His smile was at the ready. "I agree to your terms. Let's finish this."

Ofelia gritted her teeth and grabbed the door. "Let me go first." She was careful when sticking her head through the opening. She looked both ways up and down the hallway. It looked like a servants' hallway of some sort.

Sully followed her, his chest pressed to her back. He lifted his nose to search for his father again, then pointed to the right.

Ofelia wordlessly nodded and started in that direction. A waiter appeared from around the corner, a tray perched on his hand, and he gave them an odd look before continuing by. Apparently, he wasn't being paid enough to question their presence. When they turned the corner, they found another door and pushed through it.

They found a catering kitchen to their left when they emerged from the hallway. To their right, however, was another hallway, and that's where Sully pointed.

It was like being trapped in a labyrinth, Ofelia mused as they took two more corners. When they emerged at a huge open door, however, she pulled up short. There was nowhere else to go. Obviously, this was their final destination.

"You should probably come in, Ofelia," a female voice called out from inside the office. Ofelia recognized that it belonged to Celeste even though she couldn't see the other witch. "There's no sense dragging this out."

The element of surprise was long lost, so Ofelia didn't hesitate before heading into the office. She pasted a bright smile on her face—one that was so fake it almost hurt to maintain—and took a moment to glance around at her surroundings before she spoke.

"Well, *this* is an interesting group," she said as her gaze bounced between Celeste, Zeke, and Pascal. The vampire and her future father-in-law were in wingback chairs situated across from a huge mahogany desk. Celeste sat in a large leather chair there ... and she didn't look happy.

"I was just going to say the same thing to you," Celeste noted. "I mean ... what a motley crew." She shot Zeke a death glare. "It's bad manners to invade a charity event and commit murder. Don't you know that?"

Ofelia shrugged. It was such a surreal thing to say. "We all do what we have to do."

"You didn't have to do this." Celeste made a clucking sound with her tongue, as if trying to throttle back her annoyance. "It's done now, though. The question is, how are we going to end this with as little bloodshed as possible."

"I'm open to suggestions," Ofelia replied. "Oh, I know. How about you suck up the lost money, let Zeke go, and call off the mimes. I happen to think that's the best option available."

"I was just explaining that to Celeste myself when you arrived," Pascal said dryly. "She seems to feel differently."

"Zeke screwed me," Celeste fired back. "I'm not just going to sit back and do nothing. That sends the wrong message."

"And what message is that?" Ofelia queried.

"That you can hurt me and not pay the price," Celeste replied. "Zeke willfully screwed me over. If I don't make him pay, then others will think they can do it to me too."

"It's business," Zeke insisted, speaking for the first time. His face was glistening with sweat, and Ofelia could tell he was nervous to the point of passing out. "You know as well as I do that there are always risks when you get involved with business. How can you blame me when you knew what you were getting yourself into?"

"You said you had everything under control!" Celeste exploded.

"I thought I did." Zeke held out his hands and lifted his shoulders. "How was I supposed to know that some rare grackle lived there? I mean ... what are the odds?"

Celeste threw out a wall of magic, slamming the fire into Zeke's chest. He let out a thin scream as the fire threatened to consume him, but Ofelia went with her instincts and doused the flames in a split second.

"No." Ofelia vehemently shook her head when Celeste turned an incredulous glare on her. "You can't kill him. I won't allow it."

"And who says you get to decide?" Celeste demanded. "I'm the one who was screwed. I'm the one who lost my money. You can't possibly think I'm going to sit back and do nothing. That's not who I am."

Ofelia had to suck in a breath to center herself. "I get that you're upset," she started.

As if to prove her right, Celeste sent another burst of flames toward Zeke. Ofelia easily doused it a second time, causing Celeste's cheeks to flush red with fury.

"Stop doing that," Celeste gritted out.

"I can't." Ofelia opted to be rational, even though she knew that it ultimately wouldn't matter because Celeste was going to force the issue to the point of no return. There was no getting around that now, and Ofelia was resigned to it. "You know I can't." She was pleading now. "He's going to be my father-in-law. I'm not going to let you kill him."

"Even though we should because I told you to stay away from this place," Sully growled as he glared at his father.

"I was trying to help," Zeke complained. "I thought if we could come to a deal—maybe I could pay her back a portion of the money—that she would drop this vendetta. Apparently, that's not what she wants. Who knew?"

"I knew," Sully fired back. "I freaking knew, and I told you to stay away."

"There's no point in fighting about it now," Pascal pointed out. "It's done. We have to deal with the problems of the present. The issues of the past aren't important given what's going on."

Sully glowered at him. "Since when are you the voice of reason?"

"Since we have a murderous witch who will focus on killing Ofelia first to grapple with," Pascal replied. "Why do you think I'm in here? It's certainly not because I care about your father."

Realization dawned on Sully, and he felt sick to his stomach. Pascal had been trying to protect Ofelia when he sat down with Celeste. Now all of that effort was for naught. "Oh. I ... um..."

"There it is." Pascal shook his head. "Just ... shh. I'll handle this." He was calm when catching Celeste's gaze. "We're at a stalemate. I think we need to call an end to the fight and move on."

"Oh, sure." Celeste gave off the appearance of being fine with it, but there was an edge to her voice. "We'll just move on. Twenty million bucks? Who cares? Lies? Who cares?" She threw up her hands. "I won't sit back and do nothing!"

The words were barely out of her mouth before Ofelia caught a hint of movement out of the corner of her eye. The mime swooped in quickly, heading for Sully, but Ofelia threw it back against the wall and disintegrated it before it got too close.

Celeste didn't stop. She did it again. This time the mime was aimed at Zeke, however.

Ofelia ripped it to shreds before it took two steps, the remnants of the fabricated creature turning to ash as it dissipated.

"I can do this all day," Ofelia warned. "How many mimes have you got?"

"Enough so if I throw them at you all at once, you'll lose your boyfriend and Zeke," Celeste replied. She sounded sure of herself. "Your friends in the ballroom? The siren and the ... whatever he is. I can't quite get a read on him." She looked momentarily bothered. "They'll die too."

Ofelia paused with her hand in the air. She'd been about to throw a spell at Celeste to freeze her so she could bind her. That idea fled in an instant, though.

"I'll kill them all just to be declared the victor," Celeste supplied, correctly reading Ofelia's mind. "Is that what you want? Do you want to lose your friends? Do you want to lose ... *that*?" She pointed at Sully on a nose wrinkle. "He's very handsome, but he's just a shifter. You could do so much better."

"No, I couldn't," Ofelia shot back. "There is no one better."

"Give me Zeke, and we'll call it even," Celeste said. "All your friends will live to fight another day. You can move on from ... whatever this is, and we'll never speak of it again." Her tone was full of false brightness.

It made Ofelia tired just thinking about the veneer Celeste constantly had to maintain. "No," she replied simply. "We're not doing that. You can give up your vendetta against Zeke, accept that you were the one who went all-in on a stupid plan, and move on. That's your one and only option."

"And if I don't agree to your terms?" Celeste asked sweetly.

Ofelia didn't hesitate before laying it all out there. "Then I'm going to have to kill you."

Sully's insides tightened at the words, but he was secretly proud of Ofelia for delivering them in such a matter-of-fact manner. On a different occasion, she might've tried to negotiate. She obviously understood that Celeste wasn't going to allow that to be an option.

"Just like that, huh?" Celeste queried in a low voice.

"Just like that," Ofelia confirmed.

"Well, then..." Celeste didn't get up from her chair. Instead, she waved her hands and threw up a shield at the exact moment Zeke lunged at her. She seemed to be expecting the move.

Pascal was also expecting the move, because he was on his feet in the blink of an eye, and he caught Zeke before he could launch himself across the desk.

"Don't be stupid!" Pascal snapped when Zeke fought his efforts. "You'll die if she gets her hands on you."

"You're going to die anyway," Celeste fired back on a shriek. When she unleashed her magic, it came in the form of a wave of mimes. They piled into the room from multiple doors—some that were hidden behind bookcases—and they didn't discriminate when they picked a target. They were there to kill anyone and everyone.

Ofelia deflected the first wave of mimes easily enough. She managed to rip through five of them without breaking a sweat. The second line was staggered, however, and they came too fast for her to stop them.

Pascal swooped in and grabbed the first, wrapping his

hand around the creature's neck and shaking it so hard it turned to ash. He managed to punch out at another and send it into the wall. That didn't stop them from coming, however.

Ofelia caught sight of Celeste on the other side of the desk. She was grinning, as if she were watching her favorite soap opera. She didn't seem to care that real people were at risk. And that would always be the problem with Celeste, Ofelia realized.

Rather than try to stop the mimes, Ofelia threw her magic at the shield Celeste had erected. The other witch wasn't expecting the move because her eyebrows practically flew off her forehead when Ofelia made a human-sized hole in the magical bubble. Rather than climb into Celeste's safe space and go after her there, however, Ofelia put on a magical display and dragged Celeste through the opening, out into the real world.

"*Punio*," Ofelia hissed as she grabbed Celeste's hair. She wasn't a hair-puller by nature, but she recognized she had to be fast. She yanked as hard as she could, causing Celeste to cry out, and then she threw the woman against the wall before pinning her there with another spell. "*Glacio*," she hissed.

Ofelia moved fast. She gathered Zeke, Sully, and Pascal to her before erecting a shield to protect them. Then she watched with impassioned detachment as Celeste began to understand what was about to happen. Thanks to the shield, Ofelia's group was protected from the rabid mimes. Celeste was another story, however. She was out in the open and unable to tap into her magic to protect herself. That meant there was only one thing in the room for the mimes to feed on.

"Oh, geez," Sully said when he realized what was about to happen.

Ofelia turned so her cheek rested against his chest. She didn't want to see what was about to happen.

"It's okay," Sully assured her as he stroked his hand over her hair. "It's okay."

"It *is* okay," Pascal agreed. He was grim because he recognized things were about to turn bloody, but he didn't look away. "It's somehow poetic that she's going to fall victim to the creatures she created."

"What about after?" Zeke queried, swiping his forearm across his forehead to get rid of the sweat. "What are we going to do with the mimes when they're finished ... um ... eating?"

"There shouldn't be an after," Ofelia replied. Her gaze was lasered on Sully. He stared back into the fathomless depths of her eyes. There was nowhere else he wanted to look. "She created them. When she's gone, they should be gone too."

"Oh." Zeke's expression was momentarily blank. He made a disgusted face when realization dawned. "Oh."

"Yes, oh," Pascal agreed.

Celeste couldn't scream because of the spell, but Ofelia felt the moment when reality hit the other witch. Sully pulled her tight against his chest, and they waited things out. It was over relatively quickly, and when Ofelia looked up again, the mimes were nowhere to be found.

"That means any mimes she might've sent to the ballroom are gone too, right?" Zeke queried. "Everybody is safe."

"Everybody *is* safe," Pascal agreed. He focused his attention on Ofelia, who was slowly pulling away from Sully.

"That was a smart move, my dear. Allowing her creatures to end her that way ... it was poetic."

"I didn't want to have to kill her," Ofelia replied. "There was no choice, though. She wasn't going to let it go." Her chin jerked up when the office door swung open to allow Ben, Angelique, and Dora entrance.

"We were just checking," Angelique assured Ofelia. "We were trying to get to you—there were mimes all up and down the hallway—but we were having trouble fighting through them. Then they suddenly disappeared."

"That's when Dora showed up," Ben added. "She seemed to know where we should go."

"Is that her?" Dora asked Ofelia, gesturing toward what had once been a witch. Now it looked like a pile of shredded clothes.

"I let her mimes eat her," Ofelia replied.

"Nice." Dora grinned. "That was a smooth move."

Ofelia didn't like being congratulated for sitting back and doing nothing when a witch was eaten by murderous mimes, but she was too tired to put up a fight. "Should we do something about Honor and Jane?"

"We don't know how much they knew about this," Pascal replied. "We can keep an eye on them. For today, though, I think we should let it go."

Dora nodded in agreement. "I'll put people on them. Just to make sure."

"Fine." Ofelia nodded. "That makes sense."

"Awesome." Zeke pumped his fist. "I think that means it's time for a party. Let's go back to Krewe and get our drink on. I'll pay and everything."

Sully shot his father a withering look as he slid his arm around Ofelia's back. "Or I can take my fiancée home, order the food I promised her, and spend the next two days in bed."

"I vote for that option," Ofelia said.

"I have a magazine to read," Pascal replied when Zeke fixed his gaze on him. "That poor Bynes girl just can't catch a break. It's tragic really."

"You guys are zero fun," Zeke complained. "You're supposed to be celebrating."

"We *are* celebrating," Sully replied. "We're just not celebrating with you. In fact, now that this is over, I'm thinking you should return to Mom ... and your therapy."

Ofelia's eyebrows hopped. "He's in therapy?"

Sully nodded. "Apparently so."

"Voluntarily?"

"It's a strange new world, baby. We'll have to see how it goes."

"After we spend two days in bed, right?"

"Oh, definitely. That's the priority."

Ofelia snuggled close. All was right in her world again. For now at least. "I was hoping you would say that."

# 19
## NINETEEN

"I'm not doing it." Sully took one look at his reflection in the mirror, at the way Ofelia had tried to flatten his hair into floopy side bangs and shook his head. "It's just not happening."

For her part, Ofelia was over his whining. She stood in her ankle-length dress, which had a slit up to her thigh and a vee practically down to her navel and glared at her future husband. "We agreed that you're going as Gomez," she reminded him.

"We *did* agree to that," Sully confirmed. "I just didn't know it was going to involve ... this." He gestured toward his hair. "Do something else."

Ofelia narrowed her eyes. "You said—"

"Do something else with my hair," he insisted. "I'll wear whatever you want for a suit. I'll fight off anyone looking at your cleavage all night. I'll drink whatever you want and whisper sweet nothings in your ear until my lips fall off. I just can't do this with my hair."

Ofelia wanted to argue—she had a certain vision after all—but ultimately, she nodded. She understood why he hated the hairstyle. It did make him look like a bit of a doofus. "Fine. Stay here," she warned, extending a finger.

Sully remained in front of the mirror, only shrinking back when Ofelia returned with the bottle of water she used on Baron when he wouldn't stop sharpening his claws on the new couch. "What are you doing?" He sounded as if he was about to freak out.

"Just take a breath," Ofelia ordered. "I've got this." She was grumpy when she started spraying his hair. Once it was wet, however, she combed it back and parted it down the middle. She combed, and combed, and combed until she had it just right. Then she leaned back to admire her handiwork. "Pretty good, huh?"

Sully glanced at his reflection. Personally, he didn't see why he couldn't do his own hair. Despite what they'd gone through in the run-up to Halloween, Ofelia's couple's costume mania hadn't abided. If anything, once the trouble was behind them, she'd become even more manic. That meant Sully had to dig in his fingernails and hold on for the ride.

"It's great," he replied automatically.

Ofelia wasn't an idiot. She could read his disinterest as he smoothed the front of his suit. "You don't have to go," she said automatically. She didn't believe it, but she said it all the same. "It's fine. I'll go by myself." She flashed a smile that she didn't feel.

Sully's heart threatened to shred. "I said I would go," he insisted. "I meant it."

"You don't want to go, though."

Was that true? Sully had trouble deciding. Ultimately, he shook his head. "As long as we're together, I'm good. I want to do this." Just saying it out loud made him realize he meant it. "I just don't like it when you put goop in my hair."

"Fine." Ofelia held up her hands in supplication. "No more goop in your hair. Are you satisfied?"

His gaze moved to her dress. It hugged every curve. It made him want to roll her into bed and not leave their penthouse for the evening. Since he knew that wasn't an option, he merely smiled. "How are you keeping that dress in place?"

"I'm magical," she reminded him.

"Oh, see, I already knew that." He leaned in and pressed a kiss to her full red lips. He didn't care if the lipstick transferred to him in the least. "I love you ... even if you are grouchy and manic about the costumes."

Ofelia laughed, catching him off guard. "I'm not manic," she said finally.

He arched a challenging eyebrow.

"I'm not." The words were barely out of her mouth before she nudged him away from the mirror. "I have to fix my lipstick."

"Right, but you're not manic."

"I just said I wasn't manic." Ofelia's agitation was a sight to behold.

"Of course not." Sully flopped onto the bed and watched her work. He didn't care what she said, he was going to have fun with that dress later. "So, I have a quick update on Celeste if you're interested."

"Of course I'm interested." Ofelia concentrated hard as she reapplied her makeup. "Why wouldn't I be interested?"

"I thought maybe you were more interested in playing with your lipstick."

Ofelia shot him a warning look. "Keep pushing me, and I'll fix your hair with magic, and there won't be a thing you can do about it."

Sully scowled. "That was a horrible threat, Fe."

"I'm not sorry."

One look at her told him she was telling the truth. "I'll be fast," he promised. "First up, her company assets have been seized by the Feds. It seems, after she disappeared at the Celestial Cabaret without a trace, that people came out of the woodwork to report her misdeeds. An investigation has been launched into all of her business dealings."

"And we care about that why?" Ofelia queried.

"Because Jane and Honor are going to lose the apartment they stayed in because it was listed under Celeste's company name. They're going to be homeless."

"And maybe looking for payback," Ofelia surmised. "That makes sense. We'll have to keep an eye open where they're concerned."

"We will," Sully agreed. "Other than that, nobody has seen the mimes since she's been gone. That's hardly surprising from our end of things, but as you know, not everybody is aware of what happened."

"At least nobody else has died."

"There is that, and nobody else will die ... at least not from the mimes," he agreed. "Other than that, I got a call from my mother this afternoon."

Ofelia froze. The way he'd waited to tell her made her think he was about to deliver bad news. "Do I need to sit down?" she asked.

"No." He shook his head. "It wasn't that type of call. She just wanted to thank me for sending my father back to her with a new lease on life ... and a better attitude. Apparently, he's being attentive and doing all the things she wants."

Ofelia cocked her head. "How long do you think that will last?"

"I don't know. I think he's trying right now, but I also

think he's likely to lose interest in trying sooner rather than later. He won't be able to help himself."

"How does that make you feel?"

Sully didn't consider the question overly long. "I feel as if there's nothing I can do to change things, so I'm not going to get worked up about it." He was matter of fact. "My father is who he is. That's not who I want to be. I can't change him, but I can be the man I always wanted him to be."

Ofelia held his gaze. "Despite your refusal to let me do your hair how I want, you're the best man I know. I hope you realize that."

He smiled. "Baby, you're the best woman I know, so I guess we're perfect together."

She returned his smile and stood. "Are you ready to go to my high school reunion and make all those nasty girls I went through adolescence with drool?"

"Is this an actual high school reunion? You didn't mention that part before."

"It's close enough. We don't do anything normal in the Quarter, including reunions. You're ready, right?"

"As long as I have you, I'm ready for anything."

"Oh, that's cute. I'm being serious, though. I want them to take one look at you and say, 'Holy crap, Ofelia Archer is better than us and has it all.'"

Sully couldn't hold back his laugh. "Normally, I wouldn't encourage this sort of behavior, but you're too fired up not to adore. I will totally help sell the idea that you have it all ... because you do have it all, Fe."

"I know." She preened as she looked in the mirror. "I look great in this dress, huh?" she said as she ran her hands over her cleavage.

The saliva dried in Sully's mouth. "Yeah, baby, you look like every naughty dream I've ever had."

"So, let's go party it up right in the Quarter." She held out her hand. "Because, starting tomorrow, it's the offseason, and we're going to take advantage of that, too."

"I'm looking forward to both things."

Ofelia nodded. "Me, too. It's a whole new world essentially for the next few months. We might as well party it up as if we're the tourists."

"That's exactly what I was thinking too."

Printed in Great Britain
by Amazon